Christmas Eve Carnage 2

Sprinkles Lives

John Lynch

Praise for John Lynch

"John Lynch isn't here to mess around... and neither is his fiction. Every word, every sentence, is a well-placed bullseye from a sharpshooter of a writer."

— Brian Keene

To everyone going through it. I see you.

Cause let's face it baby, these days, ya gotta have a sequel!

— Stu Macher: Scream

Fuck everybody, that's on my body... Never let no one put smut up on your name... Keep your head down and work like I do.

— Kendrick Lamar

Chapter One

We have a breaking story. Heavy police and fire response were seen outside of a home on Dale Avenue. Firefighters spent hours working to put out an inferno. It is not known if anyone was home at the time of the fire.

Kirk Brian's eyelids fluttered. He shook his head, trying to rattle himself awake. He needed to sleep but he'd lost precious travel time because of the storm. Rain, shine, holiday, or nor'easter, it didn't matter, Kirk was a trucker and would get the job done and get it done on time. He reached for the volume knob on the radio, turned it up. "Sounds like someone is having a worse holiday than I am," he said, scratching his nuts.

Our source with the police department, who wishes to remain anonymous, has stated to us the fire is only the tip of the iceberg. According to our source, multiple bodies were found inside the home on Dale Avenue, apparently brutally murdered. Across the street, another body was found murdered. A minor child was found alive at the *scene of the crime and rushed to Glenwood Memorial Hospital in critical condition.*

Kirk gagged on a large chunk of Five Guys cheeseburger. He coughed, dislodging the wad of beef. Flecks of meat and grease splattered across his dashboard and windshield. "Jesus, fuck," he said, still coughing. "What kind of sick fucking world do we live in? Who does something like that on Christmas Eve? Maybe if people spent more time at church rather than looking at internet porn, the world would be a better place." Kirk himself spent plenty of time looking at internet porn. He figured the Lord would be more forgiving of that sin than he would of Kirk spending his money getting his dick sucked by some disease-infested lot lizard. A man had needs, after all.

He squinted, trying to make out the road in front of him. He reached and wiped the inside of the windshield with his forearm, his plaid shirt smearing grease across the glass rather than absorbing it. "Goddamnit," he said. It was tough enough to see even a short distance in front of his truck with the heavy snowfall. The windshield wipers weren't cut out for the rate of precipitation, which, thankfully, had slowed down the past few hours, allowing him to continue working. The entire Northeast had been pounded by the storm. A "hard pounding"—the exact words used on the news broadcast, which had made Kirk spit out his drink—and though the worst was behind the state of Rhode Island, they were still getting nailed, and weather reports indicated the snow wouldn't stop falling anytime soon.

Kirk turned the radio off; he'd had enough of that

bullshit. You couldn't even get Christmas music on the radio because the world had become such a dumpster fire. The media, in their never-ending quest for ad revenue, had actually interrupted Michael Bublé with a news story about a gruesome multiple homicide. Michael fucking Bublé! Thank God for radio apps and Bluetooth speakers. He steered the truck with the tops of his thighs while he continued scarfing down his burger with one hand and used the other hand to scroll through Spotify for some Christmas music. He pressed **<PLAY>** and his portable speaker came to life; Taylor Swift was singing about a Christmas tree farm. While it might not have the history of many Christmas songs, he considered it to be a *modern classic*. Not as popular as something like "All I Want for Christmas Is You," but not as popular didn't mean it wasn't as good.

He dropped his phone onto the passenger seat, then returned his gaze straight ahead, correcting his course back to the right side of the road. "That was a close one! I'd better be more careful. Last thing I need to do is jackknife this beast." Kirk wasn't worried about other vehicles. He'd seen a few accidents and a few cars stuck, but the governor had called a state of emergency, so most people stayed home. They didn't want to chance getting pulled over by the state police. Kirk sure as shit didn't want to risk another ticket, but he didn't have much of a choice; he was determined to get the cargo to its destination. "I guess the silver lining of those people getting murdered is that the cops are so busy dealing with that mess, they don't have time for my bullshit." He laughed. Kirk liked to think he had a morbid sense of humor. Really, he was just fucked in the head.

Kirk sucked down a mouthful of chocolate milkshake, then went back to work on his burger. He took a bite and the greasy patty slid out of the bun, falling onto his lap with a *splat*. "Son of a bitch," he yelled. The meat had landed on his leg but thankfully, had remained draped over his thigh rather than falling to the floor. It was still edible; his pants were far cleaner than the floor of his truck. He looked down at the mess and used a napkin to wipe the mustard off as best he could.

The moment Kirk was done with his latest distraction and brought his eyes back to the road, he hardly had time to register a Toyota 4Runner driving straight toward him. The two vehicles collided with each other in a horrible scream of metal on metal.

The 4Runner crumpled against the much larger eighteen-wheeler. Something flew out of the windshield, hit the grill of the large truck, and landed on the hood. The truck jackknifed and rolled over, skidding across the snowy ground before finally coming to a stop, its entire length blocking the road.

When Kirk came to, he rejoined the world with a pounding headache. He tried to open his eyes but could only see out of one of them; the other was bruised and swollen shut. His vision out of the eye he could open was blurry from the blood running down a slice along his hairline. His forehead was wet and sticky. He tried to wipe his face, but his right arm hurt like a son of a bitch, and he couldn't seem to move it. *Dislocated shoulder,* he thought. He wiped his face with his other hand and held it in front of his good eye. Christ, there was a lot of blood. He hoped it wasn't too serious. Kirk knew head wounds had a tendency to bleed more than other parts of the body, but the knowledge did little to alleviate his worries.

He undid his seat belt and tried to get out but slumped to the side. He was disoriented, and between the mental fog he was floating in from a likely concussion and his highly impaired vision, he hadn't even noticed that the truck had flipped onto its side. Kirk took a moment to get his bearings and then proceeded to climb out the driver's side window, which was now above him. Shards of broken glass poked and sliced, ripping his plaid shirt and drawing more blood. It took a while to climb out, only having one arm that was worth a damn, but he eventually succeeded and dropped to the snow-covered ground. The deep, heavy powder absorbed much of the impact, but Kirk was weak from the accident and couldn't stop himself from face-planting.

With great effort, he rose to his feet. The wet snow had quickly penetrated his clothing, leaving him freezing. The cab of the truck had been hot; Kirk typically kept the heat cranked, so he hadn't had his coat on, nor had he dressed especially warm. When he escaped the truck, he hadn't thought to grab his jacket from the passenger seat. Now, looking at the overturned vehicle, Kirk didn't think he had a whore's hope in hell of climbing *back* into the cab to retrieve the coat. Not with his arm fucked up the way it was.

Shit, what about the other driver? Fucking moron came straight at me!

Part of Kirk was pissed that the other driver came into his lane and caused the accident, but he also recognized that neither of them should have been on the road, and it just as easily could have been *him* who had caused an accident. Hell, he almost *had* crossed the yellow lines multiple times while stuffing his face instead of paying attention to the road. Whatever the cause of the other driver's mistake was irrelevant because, more than likely, the driver and any occupants of the vehicle had been turned into pink paste. You don't collide with a truck like Kirk's at that speed and walk away. He estimated the odds of finding a survivor in the 4Runner to be somewhere around 0 percent. Still, Kirk couldn't call himself a man of God if he didn't at least check on the SUV's occupants. He reached into his pocket for his phone. The sooner he called 911, the better. If the poor fuckers in the 4Runner *were* *d*ead, Kirk would be following them into the afterlife, dead of hypothermia, if EMS didn't arrive on scene soon.

The phone was gone. He'd left it on the passenger seat when he turned Spotify on. "You've gotta be fucking me," he said, shambling to the crumpled 4Runner. He hoped he could find a phone in the other vehicle. He thought it highly unlikely that whoever was in the SUV didn't have a phone with them, not in this day and age. But given the way his luck seemed to be going, Kirk didn't have to even find the phone yet to know it would either be broken or locked. But you can dial 911 with a locked phone, right?

Kirk thought about it for a moment and realized that, yes, you could make an emergency call with a locked phone. Maybe his luck hadn't completely dried up just yet. He shambled a bit quicker, but even without the pain from the accident holding him back, it was tough to walk through the snow. The roads had been plowed at some point, but the accumulation was quick, and the snow was heavy and a little higher than ankle-deep.

It took great effort, but eventually he made it to the crumpled pile of scrap metal and rubber that had, until recently, been a large SUV. Kirk shivered and tried rubbing himself with his one good arm but it was no use. He was soaked to the bone and no amount of friction would change his current circumstance.

The front of the vehicle was annihilated and looked like its front end had been torn off by an IED, not destroyed in a collision. Only the rear doors looked like they might be operational, but when he tried to open a door, it was stuck.

"Tee hee hee."

"Who's there?" Kirk asked. It sounded like a child's laughter . . . or a pedophile, only deeper. Kirk didn't know what the hell it was, but it was unnerving. Underneath the sound of the whipping wind, he thought he could hear bells jingling. He did a 360 and saw nothing but empty streets and snow.

His blood was boiling. Was someone seriously fucking with him instead of trying to help? It's not like whoever it was couldn't tell a catastrophic incident had just occurred. "Listen, you asshole, if you can't tell, I've been involved in a serious accident. So you can either come out here and help, or when I get my hands on you, I'll whoop your ass so hard your fucking head will spin," Kirk said with little conviction in his voice. He was badly hurt and if it *was* a child, the little shit would probably give him a run for his money.

The jingling again, this time closer. It sounded as if it came from the direction of his truck, but between the snowfall and impaired vision, Kirk couldn't see anything out of the ordinary.

Unless you counted the pancaked Toyota 4Runner as out of the ordinary.

The jingling again, louder. And the laughing.

"Down here, you fat fuck," a voice said.

Kirk wiped the blood from his eyes again and looked down. A green blur was trudging through the snow, headed straight for him. The thing approached, and when at last it was close enough to be recognizable through his impaired vision, his first thought was that he must be losing his fucking mind.

It was an elf. A fucking Christmas elf. Knee-high, green tunic, the damn thing even had the hat to top it off. It maneuvered through the snow, humming a Christmas tune.

"I must have really whacked my head good," Kirk said to himself.

Closer now, Kirk was able to get a better look. He wasn't wrong about it being a Christmas elf, which was somehow even worse because what he saw was some sort of horrific *doll*. A children's toy come to life. Either way, it couldn't be a good sign for his mental state. One of its arms was hanging on only by a thread of the tunic. The chest of the doll was caved in as if it had been crushed by some great force. It hobbled forward, its head stuck sideways at an angle, like a dog cocking its head when it didn't understand what its owner was asking of it. It spoke again, its jaw busted off-center and flapping around as it said, *"You need to learn how to drive, Kirk. You killed that poor cop. And you sent me flying through the windshield! Now you're on Santa's naughty list."*

This was a nightmare. He must be in the hospital, dreaming in a coma. Or maybe he was dead, because there was no fucking way an oversized Christmas doll was talking to him.

A swirl of ice crystals circled around the elf and it began to levitate, hovering a few feet above the snow. The crystals circled the imp faster, and through the sheet of ice, Kirk watched in horror as whatever damage had been done to the abomination fixed itself. Tights no longer ripped, its arm now back in place, and the head stuttered and moved like a stop-motion film until its neck was straight again and its jaw healed.

"Don't worry, Kirk. You might have killed the cop, but Sprinkles lives!" the doll said. He snapped his fingers and disappeared in the blink of an eye, the sheet of swirling ice crystals dissipating.

Kirk turned and tried to run but face-planted onto the snow. He landed on his dislocated shoulder and screamed in pain, tears welling in his eyes. He was cold, wet, and badly hurt. Kirk rose to his feet, cradling his arm.

The elf was suddenly in front of him, reappearing as quickly as he had disappeared. He was holding a pistol in both hands, the gun looking comically large in the hands of a doll. *"That silly cop left this in his car! You know, I really hate these things. They take the joy out of Christmas. They're very dangerous,"* Sprinkles said as he pulled the trigger. The firearm went off with a *bang* and the gun kicked back, hitting the elf in the face and knocking it on its ass.

"Fuck, my knee. You shot me in my fucking knee!" Kirk screamed, thrashing about in the snow.

Sprinkles hopped to his feet and tossed the gun aside. He snapped his fingers and a large, red velvet sack materialized in front of him. He lifted the flap and crawled inside, the bag expanding, growing impossibly wide and deep.

Kirk was focused on the fresh bullet wound in his leg, too busy screaming and crying to pay attention to Sprinkles, or the mechanical whirring turning into a loud purr as a small engine kicked on and roared to life.

Sprinkles emerged from the bag, floating horizontally in the air with his arms straight out, gripping the handle of a large snowblower. He floated backward, pulling the snowblower the rest of the way out of the bag. The elf wriggled his nose like a Hollywood interpretation of Santa Claus and the bag disappeared. *"He he he."* Sprinkles giggled. *"We've gotta clear out this snow, Kirk, otherwise they'll never find your body."*

"No, leave me alone, you sick fuck," Kirk screamed between sobs. "You're not real."

The blower moved forward, Sprinkles hovering behind it, still grasping the handle.

Kirk tried to crawl away but with a gunshot wound to the knee and a dislocated shoulder, he was helpless to escape.

The machine spit snow from the chute as the blades spun through the thick powder. Kirk screamed while the spinning blades began chewing his arm as the elf pushed the blower forward. There was a crunching noise as the blades and motor strained against Kirk's body, chopping up his flesh like raw meat and sending a mixture of bloodred snow, bone, and flesh spitting from the chute.

The elf sang, *"Just hear those sleigh bells jingling, ring-ting-tingling too!"* He continued pushing the blower over Kirk, who was screaming bloody murder as it continued chewing him up and spitting him out until the blades reached his skull, crushing it and tearing bone and brain apart. Kirk's body convulsed and the machine finally sputtered and stalled, leaving Kirk's corpse safe from further desecration from the shoulders down.

"Say, Kirk, you're a real party pooper. Santa is gonna be pissed if I don't kill that little bitch, Cindy. You fucked up my ride!" Sprinkles said. He trudged through the snow until he reached the overturned eighteen-wheeler. He climbed atop one of the wheels and sat, waiting for an opportunity.

It was Christmas, and if Santa's elf couldn't spend the day spreading joy, who would?

Chapter Two

Laurie Fuller navigated the treacherous storm in the Ford Explorer she'd rented at the airport. Her flight had been delayed due to the weather, and the airline offered to book her another and put her up in a hotel, but she'd declined, instead opting to rent a vehicle and brave the elements. It wasn't as bad as she expected, mostly because both Rhode Island and Massachusetts had issued state of emergency declarations shutting down state thoroughfares to allow the snow crews to do their work. Only essential personnel were allowed on the roads, and if the current state of the highways were any indication, it seemed Laurie was the only person who'd ignored the declaration and the danger of the storm. At one point she'd been lucky enough to travel behind a plow, allowing her to make great time and distance.

Even though she'd taken a do-it-yourself attitude about getting to her destination, she'd already missed out on whatever her brother-in-law, nieces, and nephew had planned for the holiday. Before her sister had passed away, the Feltcher family had been big on both Christmas Eve and Christmas Day. Laurie wasn't sure how they handled things now; she hadn't been around in years. When Courtney died, it had simply been too much for her to cope with. Both of her parents had died of cancer, followed by her only sibling. All within a few years of each other. She knew she should have stayed home—the prospect of seeing her brother-in-law and children was hurtful because they reminded her too much of Courtney—but the Feltcher family was all she had left. She was hit with a wall of grief before she'd even reached the Rhode Island state line. It made her ponder her own mortality. Her only three immediate family members had all died of cancer, so in her mind, it was only a matter of time until her clock ran out.

Laurie took the turn off the main road and began navigating the side streets, which was a nightmare because they hadn't seen the same attention as the highways and main roads. She slowed almost to a crawl and continued that way for the last half mile of the trip.

She sniffed, crinkled her nose. It smelled as if something was burning, and as she turned into the neighborhood where the Feltchers lived, Laurie noticed that not only did the smell get stronger, but the entire area seemed to be far brighter than it should be for this time of day.

One block away and the picture grew frighteningly clear. Her heart sank in her chest. An orange glow and black smoke appeared to be coming from the first house on Dale Avenue. "Oh my God, please let everyone be okay," she said.

The street was blocked off by police SUVs and a fire engine was parked in front of her sister's house, a steady stream of water battling the flames. The house was a mess; the roof was caved in, and entire portions of it seemed to have turned into little more than smoldering ruins. The blackened remains of the home stood in stark contrast to the white powder covering the neighborhood.

Laurie parked her car in front of the police vehicles, opened the door, and ran toward the house as fast as she could, her legs kicking up plumes of snow. She ran across the blockade and onto the front lawn before an officer finally cut her off, his arms held out in front of him. She tried to get by but he wrapped his arms around her, preventing her from getting any closer. His uniform was covered in ash, and she could feel the warmth from the blaze on his clothing and in the air around them warming her cold cheeks.

"Miss," the officer said, "you can't be here. This is an active crime scene."

"A crime scene? What happened? I came home to surprise my family but my flight was delayed."

"Family? What's your name? The detective assigned to the investigation is going to want to speak to you at the station as you're the only family member left."

Laurie grabbed the officer's face between both hands, her fingers gripping the back of his skull. The man's hat fell to the ground, burrowing into the deep snow. "What the hell are you talking about, 'the only family member left'? Did they all die in the fire? How could that happen?

Oh, please don't tell me Jack forgot to change the batteries in the smoke detector."

The officer gently pulled her hands from his face and ushered her toward one of the vehicles blocking the road. "Miss, please, I can't comment on an ongoing investigation. But the detective assigned to the case will tell you everything she can, and it is imperative that she speak with you."

Laurie allowed herself to be led to the back of one of the police vehicles, despite its intimidating appearance and her general dislike for any authority figure. She'd grown up in both a military and law enforcement family, spent her life rebelling against men in uniform and now here she was, being led by a man in a uniform, on her way to speak to a woman wearing one.

Chapter Three

Liosha Valerio had only been at work for a few hours, but already it felt like she'd done a fourteen-hour stint. She'd always worked the graveyard shift and preferred it ever since graduating from nursing school. Her body had never truly adjusted to the hours and there were plenty of times she stumbled about her home in a zombie-like shuffle, but the graveyard shift at the hospital felt like where she was meant to be. Liosha loved her job and loved taking care of her patients. Being on the overnight shift allowed her to do that, while also preventing her from having *too many* of her coworkers around. Not that she disliked her peers, but she found the more people you were around, the more bullshit you were subject to dealing with, and Liosha was at a point in her life where she liked to keep the bullshit to a minimum.

The hospital was a mess. The storm had been one for the record books. Power outages, injuries, vehicle accidents, etc.

Evenings like these were tough and at times, made Liosha consider switching to the morning shift, or maybe even second shift. At least that way there would be more personnel on staff to tackle things when the shit hit the fan. Hell, nights like tonight would have her so stressed out she'd leave work in tears, popping Ativan just to survive.

Luckily, the bulk of the patients were on the other floors. Liosha was fine with that. Sometimes it was nice to let others deal with things.

But then patients like that poor little girl would show up and Liosha was reminded of why she got into the field to begin with.

Sitting at the nurses' station, alone with her thoughts, Liosha zoned out. Her mind conjured a slideshow of images, filling in the unknowns of what Cindy had experienced based on what she saw of the little girl's trauma. The cops were tight-lipped due to the ongoing investigation. All she knew for sure was that the suspect was dead, and they may never know the details of what had been done to her after her family was slaughtered. That was all well and good because someone who would do that to a child deserved to die, but Liosha wished the fucker had been caught alive. That way, he could rot in prison before dying a horrible death.

She rubbed her palms against her eyes, her cheeks moist. Anytime a child came in as a victim of abuse, she had to fight to keep it together. Especially little girls—it hit too close to home, forcing her to think about her little Yanira.

At the end of the hall, a terrible wailing echoed

through the corridor, pulling Liosha from her thoughts before she had a chance to spiral out of control. She pushed herself out of her chair and ran to Cindy Feltcher's room.

Cindy's eyes fluttered, vision blurry. Her mind was in a fog and her body didn't seem to respond to her attempts to move. She focused, trying to sit up, but the moment she moved, her entire body lit up in pain, her entire central nervous system on fire. She screamed bloody murder and weakly thrashed her arms about, tangling them in the rat's nest of wires and tubes running along her body attached to various medical machines beeping and booping from the side of her bed.

A nurse ran into the room and helped clear the wires from her. "*Shhh*, hunny, you're okay. You're at the hospital now. You're safe and everything is gonna be all right."

Cindy still howled, sobbing from both the physical and emotional pain she'd endured. When she'd first woken, she only knew she hurt and was alone. But as the fog cleared, the memories of Christmas Eve returned. Dad, Adam, and Katy . . . all dead. Even their friends and cat had been brutally murdered. She had tried to tell the cop who rescued her about the crazy elf but the trauma of having her teeth ripped out left her unable to speak clearly, and the cop misunderstood what she'd been trying to tell him. Instead of destroying Sprinkles, he had saved the toy from the inferno.

She wished the cop had never found her. Why couldn't Sprinkles have finished her off? Now she was all alone.

The nurse hugged her tight, whispering softly in her ear, "*Shhh*, you're okay now. My name is Liosha, and I'm not going to let anyone else hurt you."

Cindy sobbed against the woman's shoulder, grateful for the nurse's kindness. When the sobs died down, no longer racking her body, she tried to speak but it came out a garbled mess and hurt so bad that she began to cry again.

"Baby, you can't talk right now. You're missing a lot of teeth and it's going to be painful for a few days. Don't try right now. Here, let me get you something to write with."

Liosha tried to pull away, but Cindy gripped her tightly. She didn't want to be alone. Despite her being a stranger, the nurse's physical closeness comforted Cindy. Not to mention, it was still dark outside. Dark in her room. Dark in the halls. Cindy didn't want to be alone in the dark, not when Sprinkles was out there.

"You're okay. I'm just going to get you something to write with. That way, you don't have to try to talk. I promise I'll be right back," Liosha said, gently pulling herself free from Cindy's death grip.

Cindy watched as Liosha left the room, her heart pounding in her chest as the nurse's pink scrubs and bobbing ponytail were the last thing she saw before she was alone again. The woman's soft voice and slight accent, along with her warm embrace, had calmed her. Now her mind raced a mile a minute.

She heard a noise in the corner of the room and quickly looked in the direction it came from. She wished it weren't so dark. Even the glow of the television would make things better. Or her phone—the flashlight would definitely make her feel safer. Of all the things the cop had saved for her, he grabbed the damn elf and not her phone. She always heard grown-ups talking about how kids these days couldn't last ten minutes without being glued to their phones. A stupid thing old people said to talk down about something they didn't understand. They hadn't grown up interacting with technology the way that children today do.

Now, alone in the dark, Cindy yearned for her phone the way her lungs yearned for oxygen. Maybe they *were* right. But who cares? The world changes, times change. There were so many things she could do with it just to keep her mind off the dark. With her phone, it wouldn't *be* dark. The glow of the screen and the flashlight would make sure of that.

The noise again in the corner. Cindy pushed herself up and laboriously scooted backward until she was sitting up against the headboard, pushing the hard plastic into the wall. Sprinkles was here, back to finish the job. Suddenly she didn't wish the freak show had killed her. She didn't want to die, even though she did miss her family.

She screamed again. Being brave hadn't worked. Why did Liosha leave her? Tears ran down her cheeks. She was hurt, alone, and afraid. And there was something wrong with her foot; it didn't feel right. It hurt, but parts of it felt different and she couldn't explain it.

Liosha returned, this time flicking on the wall switch as she entered the room. It was only the dim lights, but the additional luminance helped to push back the terror Cindy felt, and then the tension started rolling off her in waves.

The little girl pointed at the corner of the room and Liosha turned to see what she was pointing at. She shook her head, a confused look on her face. "Here, write on this," she said.

Cindy took the pad and pen, scribbled on it, flipped it around, then handed it to Liosha.

Heard noise in the corner. Couldn't see. Dark.

A clicking noise in the corner jolted Cindy upright.

"Was that the noise, hunny?" Liosha asked.

Cindy nodded, her eyes wide with terror.

"Oh, you poor girl," she said, "that was the air conditioner. The unit pumps out the heat to the room, so it turns on and off every now and then, that's all." She walked over to the unit and patted it. "These old things are always clicking and whirring. You'll get used to it."

Cindy slumped her shoulders. She didn't want to get used to it. She didn't want to be here. What had she ever done to deserve to spend her Christmas in a hospital, all of her family dead?

Liosha handed Cindy the pad. "What's wrong?"

Sprinkles.

Liosha furrowed her brow. "Sprinkles? I don't get it, baby."

The elf. Where is he? Cop grabbed him from the fire.

Liosha looked at the paper, confused, before her eyes lit up as if she understood what Cindy meant. "You want your toy? Hunny, they brought you in an ambulance. There was no cop here, and you didn't have any toys with you. I can see if we have something for you at the nurses' station. We held a toy drive here recently, and there may be something left over."

"*Mmm, mmm,*" she mumbled, shaking her head side to side. No Christmas toys. Nothing. She never wanted to see an elf, or anything to do with Christmas ever again. She scribbled on the pad.

Where is the cop? Sprinkles is still out there. Don't let him hurt me.

Liosha read the paper again. Cindy watched the wheels turning in the woman's head.

"I'll call the station for you, baby. If they have your toy, I'll go down and get it myself once the roads are better," the nurse said. A tear rolled down Liosha's cheek and she wiped it away. "I promise I won't let anyone hurt you."

A beeping noise came from somewhere in the hallway. Liosha turned her head toward the noise before looking back at Cindy. "I have to go check on one of my other patients. I'm here all night. If you need me, just press the red button, and if I'm not busy, I'll come right away. I promise you're okay now," she assured, walking toward the door. Liosha stopped in the doorway and went to turn the light off, then stopped. She must have seen the look of terror in Cindy's eyes because instead of flicking the switch, she said, "I'll leave these on for you, but try to get some rest."

Though the room was no longer pitch-black, it didn't change the fact that Cindy was alone again.

And somewhere in the dark, Sprinkles was loose.

Liosha left the old man's room and peeled off her latex gloves. The stubborn bastard had been pulling at his IV again. In a way, she was thankful for the old coot's disruption because if she'd stayed with Cindy any longer, she would have broken into tears herself, and that wouldn't do at all. Stability for her patients, being a rock for them to lean on when they were weak—for Liosha, those were points of pride, things she could provide for them, which, in turn, was a boon to her own mental health. Ever since her daughter had been taken away from her, Liosha took solace in easing the pain and suffering of others. It was a way for her to feel important after having felt powerless for far too long.

It had been years ago that Yanira was taken from her, but she never forgot, never stopped hurting. She'd been at work, bussing tables at the local Chelo's. The pay was crap, but the tips were good. Many of the locals stopped in a few days a week and as she became friendly with them on a more personal level, they stopped in more often and left better tips. Eventually, her Thursday through Saturday night shifts were enough to pay the bills, buy some nice things, and squirrel some money away.

But one night, her babysitter had canceled on her last minute, leaving her high and dry. She didn't want to call out of work; she'd only recently returned from a worker's compensation injury and didn't want her boss to be upset because she was already calling in sick after having been out for so long. He'd been as understanding as required by law for the injury, but when it came to last-minute call outs, she knew she might as well phone him and quit because she wouldn't have a job the next day, regardless.

In a bind, she'd asked her upstairs neighbor, Joe, if he could keep an eye on Yanira so she could go to work. Joe wasn't someone she'd considered a friend, but she knew him well enough. Or at least, she thought she did. What could go wrong? It wasn't like she was doing a double, just an eight and out. Besides, her little Yanira was no baby, she was eight years old. A big girl and independent for her age. But when Liosha arrived home from work, she knew something was off. Joe was nowhere to be found and she discovered Yanira's little body brutally beaten, crumpled in the corner of the living room. When the police arrived on the scene, they'd discovered Joe naked in his bathtub with a self-inflicted gunshot wound to the head. A suicide note left in his apartment described, in too much detail, that he'd done it because he was getting urges again. That Yanira's young body was too much of a temptation, and the only way he'd been able to push the urges away was to brutalize her so her childish looks no longer held sway over him. He understood he was a monster but no way would he be going back to Glenwood Correctional Institute. He'd rather die.

If she hadn't seen it with her own eyes, if it hadn't happened to her own daughter, she'd have never believed it. Joe was so nice. She had never noticed anything odd about him, no weird looks or bad vibes, but when the Glenwood Police Department began to investigate further, they soon discovered that Joe Stanfield didn't exist. His real name was Henry Cooper, and he had served fifteen years for child molestation. Upon release, Cooper registered as homeless, using the local shelter's address, effectively skirting the automated phone calls that should have gone out to notify his neighbors.

Liosha had been devastated, as any mother would. Her baby was taken from her by a sick, disgusting excuse for a man, and she had been powerless to intervene. For a while, things had been touch and go. She had been depressed, angry, and mentally spiraling. She'd even attempted suicide on more than one occasion, but God had never seen fit to take her.

That was when she turned the corner. She knew she had been saved for a reason, but a second chance would only go so far if she didn't pick herself up and make the effort to do better. Like her mother told her as a child, "God helps those who help themselves." She found a therapist who helped, then eventually decided to put herself through nursing school. Helping others in need was just the thing *she* needed.

She'd briefly considered becoming a cop but in the

end, decided it would be better to help people who needed it rather than pursue justice after the fact.

After all that, despite what her therapist told her and still tells her, she needed to find it in her heart to forgive herself. And now, seeing Cindy beaten and bedridden brought back all the bad memories and feelings.

Liosha popped her head in to check on Cindy, who was now asleep, tossing fitfully in her nightmares.

Chapter Four

Laurie sat in a private room at the station, chewing her nails. The room was sterile and cold, much like an interview room—at least those she'd seen on television shows. And why the hell was it so cold, anyway? It was wintertime; did the city not want to waste money on turning the heat up? Was she a suspect and they were trying to make her uncomfortable? Based solely on what she had seen on TV and film, she thought that might be the case. How could they see her as a potential suspect? Her mind raced a million miles a minute trying to figure it out. The only real reason she could think of was the fact that she'd shown up to the scene of a crime claiming to be a family member. But it was Christmas, what was so suspicious about showing up to a family member's home during the holiday season?

The more her mind ran wild debating whether or not they might consider her a suspect, the more she didn't want to be sitting there in the room alone. The officer on scene had convinced her to allow them to escort her to the station, dangling the prospect of information in front of her like a carrot.

Just when Laurie had bitten to the end of her last fingernail, a tall woman walked through the door and stood opposite her. Her brunette hair was just past shoulder-length, and she wore jeans and a plaid shirt with the sleeves rolled up. Laurie was instantly reminded of a character—Deb—from her favorite television show, *Dexter*.

The two women locked eyes for a moment before the detective spoke, "Why are you looking at me like that?" she asked.

Taken aback, Laurie didn't know what to say, so she kept quiet. Not how she expected this to start.

"You're making a face at me, that's why I'm asking. Do I have shit on my face or something?"

"Yeah . . . I mean, no, you don't have anything on your face. I didn't mean to look at you weird, just . . . when you walked in the door, you looked familiar."

The woman laughed. "Yeah, I get that a lot. My name is Jennifer. You can call me Detective Moore or Jennifer, doesn't matter to me. Before you ask, no, you're not a suspect. Figured I'd get that out of the way before you chew your fingers down to the bone," she said, using her head to motion at Laurie's hands.

Laurie looked down at her fingers. She hadn't realized she'd been biting her nails and was now embarrassed at how she'd gone to town on them. She clasped her hands together and squeezed them between her thighs.

"So . . . Miss Fuller, right?" Detective Moore asked.

"Yes, that's right."

"Good. So, Miss Fuller, what I'm going to tell you is going to be very tough to hear. Late last night, a call was placed from a phone which was traced by nine-one-one as having come from the residence on Dale Avenue. Your brother's house, correct?"

"Brother-in-law, but yes, that is correct."

"The nine-one-one operator had not been able to speak to the caller, but what they heard on the phone was enough for them to send a police response to the scene. When Officer Durgin arrived, he discovered multiple deceased individuals and the home ablaze."

Laurie's eyes went wide. She knew it had to have been bad for her to be sitting here like this, but she was still shocked when the words left Detective Moore's lips.

"They all died in the fire?" Laurie asked.

Detective Moore shook her head. "No, not everyone. And the fire was not the only tragedy that took place at the residence."

"Not everyone? So, who? And what are you talking about, 'not the only tragedy'?"

"Miss Fuller, I'm sorry to have to tell you this, but only your niece, Cindy, survived. And she was badly injured."

How? How could something like this have happened on Christmas Eve? Laurie broke down. It was too much. Far worse than she had expected. She cried for what felt like hours before Detective Moore continued.

"Laurie, they didn't die in the fire. There was another man there. An ex-convict named Chad Reynolds. We spoke to the prison where your brother-in-law, Jack, worked. We have reason to believe the man targeted him and killed everyone in the house. We also believe he murdered the neighbor across the street. We're not sure about the specifics and forensics is going to have a fucking awful time recreating this scene—it doesn't make any sense—but the best we can figure is that Jack killed the man responsible while also suffering a fatal injury. Cindy survived, but she was tortured. According to the staff I spoke with at the hospital, she's going to pull through . . . physically, at least."

Hearing Jack spoken about in the past tense was too much and Laurie lost it again. Jack, Adam, Katy . . . all gone. The entire family her sister had built, murdered. All but their youngest daughter.

Detective Moore waited for Laurie to finish crying. "So what now?" Laurie asked, wiping her eyes.

"Well, we just wanted to see if there was anything you could add. We *think* the scumbag responsible for this had a bone to pick with Jack, but we're not sure. We're working with Glenwood Corrections to determine what sort of insight they can give us."

Laurie knew that couldn't be all they wanted. What could she possibly tell them about Jack's enemy issues at the prison? It's not like he spoke about stuff like that with her. They hardly ever talked, much less discussed his job.

Detective Moore sat in the chair across from Laurie, made a tent with her hands. "And there is the matter of Cindy . . . she's your next of kin. I know this is a lot to take in right now, but in the next few days there are going to be a lot of people from many different places, including the hospital she is staying at and state social workers, who are going to want to speak with you."

"Why would they want to speak with me?" Laurie asked, too stunned to understand what Detective Moore was *really* saying.

"Laurie, to put it bluntly, the hospital is going to be looking to collect whatever money they can for treatment. And being that you're Cindy's next of kin, child services is going to be looking to either place her with you or place her somewhere else. Like I said, this is a lot to take in, and nobody is trying to tell you what to do, but these things are going to come up sooner than you'd think."

So there it was, the catch. Laurie knew the detective was right. Bill collectors were ruthless, and at the end of the day, whether Laurie wanted a child or not, *someone* was going to have to step up and take responsibility for the only surviving member of the Feltcher family. In a perfect world, there would be time to make such life-altering decisions. But in a perfect world, her entire family wouldn't have been brutally murdered. You couldn't choose the pieces on your chessboard, but you had agency over the moves you made with the ones you did have. Laurie didn't want a kid and didn't have the first clue about raising a child. She had no motherly instincts to trust, but these were the pieces in play. Even so, there was only one *real* choice, so she made it.

"I'll take her. She should be with family. I don't know how we're gonna make this work, but what choice do I have? I can't let my niece get bounced around by the system."

Detective Moore nodded, a warm smile lighting up her face. "Laurie, you're doing the right thing. I can't imagine what you're going through, and I'm sure this is going to be a massive change in your life, but for that little girl, for Cindy, it's probably the only choice where she has a real shot. Something like this is going to leave a mark on a kid, stain them for the rest of their lives. And the system is no place for a child her age. The sad truth is that families don't want older kids. They want babies. Little boys and girls her age get bounced around from home to home, if they're lucky. But most of them end up in group homes, and the reality of the situation is that those places are not ideal settings for a little girl to grow up and thrive. They're a setup for failure."

"When can I see her?" Laurie asked.

"Soon. The roads are pretty bad right now. We can get you there, but the hospital is currently running on generators because of the storm. They're not gonna allow visitors during this time of the morning even if they weren't dealing with the outage. But, I'm going to do my best to get you there as soon as possible. I'll make sure the necessary calls get made to the state, let them know about your intent to take on guardianship of Cindy, and I'll see what's going on at the hospital. If I have to, I'll use my peace officer status to get you in there to see her. It's not like their security staff is going to stop me."

"Thank you, Detective Moore."

"Please, call me Jennifer."

"Okay, Jennifer." Laurie smiled.

"So, we've got some time to kill before the roads are cleared and we can get you to the hospital. I'll get you some food and coffee, and I also took the liberty of having an officer drive your rental to the station. I didn't want you to have to go back to your brother-in-law's house."

"I really appreciate it. You're right, I don't want to see that place again."

Jennifer nodded and motioned for Laurie to follow her. There was nothing good about anything that had happened, but at least she left the interview room confident she wasn't going to get pinned for a crime she didn't commit. And despite her reservations about being a parental figure, she was anxious to get to her niece.

I can't wait for Christmas to be over, she thought.

Chapter Five

Anthony Ramsdell sat behind the wheel of the ambulance, eyes steady on the road, dick hard as a rock in his pants. His partner, Kendra, had been rubbing his thigh the entire trip, telling him about all the things she'd love to do to him. It was a game she played with him, and though he played along, it was starting to piss him off that she was such a relentless cocktease. She'd been doing it for months, and maybe she really wanted him, maybe she didn't. He wasn't sure because, for whatever reason, every time she got to behaving like this, he never tried to push it any further. Still, even if he wasn't getting it in, he welcomed the attention.

But this wasn't a good time for her to be teasing him. The roads were atrocious, and he had enough trouble keeping control of the ambulance before she started diverting the blood from his brain and sending it straight to his prick. They needed to get this sad sack in the back of the vehicle to Glenwood Hospital. Once they'd dropped off the package, he would be free to play with *his* package.

The man in the back of the ambulance was a prisoner at the high-security compound of Glenwood Department of Corrections, and this was the third time in as many months that Anthony had driven the man to the hospital. They'd gotten the call not long ago: reported chest pains. The inmate, Keith Filmore, was known to self-inflict wounds and to fake life-threatening conditions in order to take furloughs. And considering the state didn't want to take the risk of having a dead inmate on their hands, the prison medical staff sent Anthony out to cover their own asses. The man was doing life, and such situations were typically the only time he'd get to see the world beyond the razor wire. Last month, Keith had shoved an entire pencil up his cock. Anthony thought the staff at the prison were bullshitting him, but Keith had happily dropped his pants and said, "Now I really am a pencil dick."

The officer riding in the back of the ambulance with Keith locked eyes with Anthony. "Dollars to donuts, there's nothing wrong with this piece of shit. The medical staff back at the prison just keeps sending these guys out for two reasons. Some of them are bleeding hearts who don't know how to tell these guys to suck it up, you're in prison, shit's not supposed to be fun. The rest of them? Scared to death of lawsuits. These pussies will sue for anything now. Fucking guys don't know how to do time like real convicts anymore. And then you've got the sleazeball ambulance-chasing attorneys who are nothing but bottom feeders, taking any case they can in hopes of a big payoff. The whole system, a bunch of fucking enablers from the top down."

Anthony nodded in agreement. Not that he agreed, he really had no idea what the hell went on in the prison. He'd heard a lot of the same rhetoric from many of the officers, so it probably had at least *some* truth to it, but it was hard to tell what was true and what was complaint coming from a disgruntled law enforcement officer. He had half a mind to believe that most of the staff saw the inmates as subhuman. They certainly spoke about them that way. And as far as Keith faking the chest pains? Anthony couldn't say for sure; that one was really a toss-up. Wouldn't be the first time, and it sure as shit won't be the last. But fuck, did he really have to fake it during the worst snowstorm the state had seen in a decade?

Now that Anthony thought about it, the situation was pissing *him* off. That son of a bitch better be about to die since he was out here risking his life to transport him. Because if he found out the man was faking it, the next time he had to pick his bitch ass up, he'd kill the fucker himself.

Keith grunted in the back. "Officer Smythe," he croaked.

Officer Smythe leaned forward. "What do you want, you malingering piece of dog shit?"

Anthony grimaced, trying not to shoot a load in his boxers as his partner rubbed him over his pants. He looked in the rearview mirror again, right on time to see Keith snort a mouthful of snot and spit a loogie on Officer Smythe's face.

Without a second wasted, the lawman retaliated,

driving his fist against Keith's jaw. Anthony flinched at the sound of bone on flesh.

"He ain't faking that one, nasty motherfucker," Officer Smythe said as he wiped the green glob of phlegm from the bridge of his nose with his uniform sleeve. "Hey, Anthony. He tried to attack you, right?"

"No, what the hell are you talking about?" Anthony shook his head.

"I had to subdue the inmate because when you were getting him situated, he tried to bite you, right?"

"Oh, yeah. Yeah, you're right," Anthony said, realizing that Officer Smythe intended to lie his way out of assaulting the inmate. He didn't want to get involved in that kind of shit. Why couldn't they just have a nice, quiet shift? One where nobody got punched in the face, nobody died, and Kendra finally sat on his dick. That sounded like a good day to him.

"Stop!" Kendra yelled from the passenger seat, slamming her hands on the dashboard.

Anthony stomped on the brake, sending the ambulance skidding toward an overturned eighteen-wheeler. He'd been too busy watching Officer Smythe and Filmore's exchange in the back. He then cut the wheel to the left which made the situation worse, sending the vehicle fishtailing. Two of the wheels left the road and Anthony sucked wind through his teeth. "Hang on," he said, bracing for a rollover. When it seemed all but inevitable that the ambulance would flip, gravity impossibly took over and the wheels hit the asphalt once more. The ambulance skidded to a stop as the side of the vehicle hit the eighteen-wheeler with much less force than Anthony expected.

"Holy fucking shit!" Kendra exclaimed, letting out a deep exhale.

Anthony gripped the wheel, his heart pounding in his chest so hard he felt his pulse throbbing in his ears. "That was fucking insane," he said.

"You dipshit, didn't they teach you how to drive?" Officer Smythe scolded, peeling himself off the floor between the stretcher and the rear bench seat, where he'd somehow managed to fall.

"Of course, asshole. I know how to drive. But look at this shit! It came out of nowhere!"

Officer Smythe looked up to see what Kendra and Anthony were already staring at—an eighteen-wheeler jackknifed across the road and what was left of the vehicle that had the misfortune of colliding with it.

"Kendra, we gotta go see if they need our help."

Kendra sighed. "Ugghhh, I don't want to go out there."

"You better not fucking do it," Officer Smythe said. "We can't stop to help these people, it's against policy. This guy can *only* go to the hospital and back. I'm not losing my job so you can play hero. Whoever is in there is dead. Look at that mess."

Anthony didn't care what Smythe had to say. He understood where the man was coming from—the prison had policies, and their employees were required to follow them—but Anthony didn't work for the prison, and he wasn't subject to their policies. He worked for a private ambulance transport company that paid him slightly more than minimum wage—not enough to deal with assholes like Smythe. Frankly, he didn't give a flying fuck if the officer would be disciplined for Anthony's decision to stop. It was the right thing to do.

Anthony hopped out of the ambulance, and Kendra followed. The flurries were still coming, though not as hard as before. Visibility remained tough, given the pure white landscape and the falling precipitation. They trudged a few feet in the snow. When they were closer to the wreck, Anthony noticed large areas of red staining the snow. "Jesus, someone must have gotten turned to pink mist from the crash," he said.

"Someone has to be really fucked-up from this kind of shit. It's kinda cool," Kendra replied.

Anthony looked at her and shook his head. "You're one morbid bitch, huh?"

"You'll thank me later."

Anthony felt a little stirring in his pants. He wasn't 100 percent sure what she meant, but if it was in the ball-park of what he *thought* she meant, he was about to be one happy camper. "Okay, let's check it out. See if anyone needs our help, and if not, we can just call it in. I don't think anyone has reported it yet. This strip is nothing but fast-food joints and stores that are closed because of Christmas and the storm, so if we're the first to drive by, there's a good chance nobody even knows about this."

"You know, I think you're right," Kendra said, "I've never been the first one on the scene of something like this before. It's kind of a rush."

It was a rush, sure, but Anthony wasn't turned on by

it because he wasn't a sicko. Clearly Kendra had a few screws loose, but hey, if he could benefit from it, who was he to complain?

"Hey, what's that?" Kendra pointed past the truck.

Anthony looked where she was pointing, and just past the big rig, near the unfortunate, crumpled SUV, was a large red . . . something. It was hard to tell from this distance; it simply looked like a giant red blob. "I'm not sure. I can't climb on this truck, though. I'm gonna look through the windshield and see what I can see. Maybe there's someone in there. You go check out the other vehicle."

Kendra smiled. "Okay, gotcha. I'll holler if I need you."

Anthony watched Kendra as she left, a shroud of snow soon masking her. He peered inside the cab.

No driver to be seen.

But there was a creepy doll. A horrible interpretation of a Christmas elf. Its green tunic was bright but had dark splotches all over it. The thing's face was a weird gray, like a gravestone. And it had these large eyes the color of the moon at night. There were cracks in the face that looked almost like healed scars, if a toy could have such a thing.

"Wow, what kind of grown-ass man drives around with something like that? Guy must be a pedo or something," Anthony said to himself.

A voice on the wind. " . . . ome here," it said.

"What? Kendra? Did you find something?"

It was her, louder this time. "Come here!"

Anthony pushed off the hood of the overturned truck

and booked it in the direction of Kendra's voice.

"You've gotta see this shit," she yelled.

Ahead, Anthony could see she was standing beside the big red blob, which, as he drew closer, he saw was a massive snowblower. By far the largest one he'd ever seen.

He slowed to a jog, then a walk, stopping a few steps from Kendra. He hadn't been sure what the big deal was, why she wanted him to see a snowblower, but as soon as he'd gotten close, he soon realized it wasn't *just* the snowblower she was calling him over to see. No, they were standing smack-dab in the middle of the most horrific scene either of them had ever arrived at. He was hesitant to call it a murder, but he couldn't think of any other suitable scenario.

Blood drenched the snow in the surrounding area. The storm had covered up some of the gore with fresh powder, but in the immediate area, large pools of scarlet dominated the splotches of white. The crumpled vehicle was also painted red and had flecks of pink and gray that Anthony couldn't identify, but he knew they had to be chunks of organic matter that hadn't been completely chopped up by the blades of the snowblower.

Worst of all was the mess at the front of the machine. It had to be the biggest snowblower he'd ever seen that *wasn't* industrial-sized. A torso, stained red and soaked with both blood and snow, was lodged in the blades.

Kendra examined the corpse, focused intently on the carnage.

Anthony moved closer to get a better look. From mid chest up, what was left of the body was nothing more than a frothy mess of pink goop, the snow having mixed with the blood and organic matter. Partially chopped up bits of bone and muscle tissue floated around in the soupy mess, and strings of flesh and sinew were wrapped around the large blades.

"This is fucking sick," Kendra said.

"Yeah, definitely." Anthony didn't think she meant sick, as in disgusting. She gazed at the mess the way a horny teenager stared at the first piece of porn he stumbled across. Awe plastered on her face as if she'd had a life-changing experience.

"We gotta call this in," Anthony said.

"Okay, yeah. I don't know what happened here aside from the accident. There's a body in the 4Runner, obviously dead, and there is this guy here. But it doesn't explain anything about what the fuck happened."

"Leave it to the cops. We can't do any—" he stopped short of finishing his sentence, shocked as Kendra walked around the scene snapping pictures with her phone. He let her do her thing, choosing to ignore the morbid behavior. Maybe it was some sort of weird kink. He pulled out his own phone and called 911, alerting emergency services of the accident. When he finished the call, he placed his phone back in his pocket and said, "Hey, the fire department and police are on their way. I told them we've gotta transport this inmate to Glenwood Hospital so we can't stay on scene. We're probably going to have to wait at the hospital to talk to someone. Let's get the fuck outta here."

Kendra looked at him over her shoulder, flashed a smile. "Okay, I'm done anyway. Let's go."

They trudged back to the ambulance. Anthony could hear Officer Smythe yelling something, though he didn't really care what the man was saying. Not far behind the ambulance, Anthony saw a set of flashing lights through the shroud of falling snow. It was Officer Smythe's partner, whose job was to follow the ambulance in a department vehicle. He was sure the guy was as pissed as Smythe. Oh well, they could both go fuck themselves.

Anthony stopped quickly to peek through the windshield of the eighteen-wheeler again, just to be sure he hadn't somehow missed a body, or the driver hadn't been moving around somehow.

The cab was empty.

Anthony had a nagging feeling that something about the big rig was off. He was tired and thought maybe the messy scene had rocked him a bit. He completely forgot about the elf doll that had been sitting in the cab the first time he'd peered into the vehicle.

Sprinkles clung to the undercarriage of the ambulance, his grip unwavering. A living doll, his toy body knew no limits. He didn't feel exhaustion, never grew tired. Sprinkles would hold on as long as necessary; there was still a job to do. That little bitch child had survived, and if Sprinkles didn't finish what he'd started, well . . . let's just say Santa isn't so fucking jolly these days. He got lucky when the fat bastard in red had given him life once more, albeit in this ridiculous body. If he failed, there was no telling what the consequence would be.

As he clung to the undercarriage, the driver somehow managed to hit every speed bump along the way, even with the mounds of powder on the road. With the impact of each one, Sprinkles grew angrier, his urge to murder now commensurate with his rage. His body still felt pain, though pain couldn't stop him. A sick joke from the big man, no doubt.

From above, Sprinkles heard the driver of the ambulance roll down the window. "Ugghhh, this coffee is too hot," a voice said as a stream of steaming hot, brown liquid flew out the window, the force of the vehicle in motion sending the beverage underneath the ambulance, splashing the elf's entire face.

"I'm gonna kill that naughty son of a bitch," Sprinkles said, thankful there were no cactus farms around for the driver to barrel through.

Chapter Six

Back upstairs at the police station, Laurie sipped her coffee amid the hustle and bustle of the station. It was Christmas morning, but the department was *not* running short-staffed today. Between the normal problems of a winter storm being escalated due to the severity of the nor'easter and the tragedy that had befallen her family, Glenwood Police Department was all hands on deck. Detective Moore had mentioned a few officers had even gotten called in from home. Laurie figured they must be pretty pissed about that. She couldn't imagine how she'd feel sitting at home opening presents, then the station calls and tells you to leave your family and get your ass into work or face a suspension.

Was that what Jack's job had been like? She knew he worked a lot of shifts and on many holidays, often complaining about how he wanted to be home with the family but couldn't. Before her sister died, she used to complain to Laurie about him being held over on holidays. Why would anyone want to work these jobs for shit pay, shit hours, and then be forced to endure the mental stress of the job and what it does to their families?

Laurie made her own schedule as a Certified Public Accountant. Things got busy during tax season, sure, but for most of the year, she had a steady clientele that kept her busy but wasn't so demanding that she lived at work. Not that living at work would have made any difference to her quality of life. Laurie spent most of her days wallowing in sorrow. With both her parents and her sister dead, she would spend long periods of time staring into space, counting the hours until her own demise. If life taught her anything recently, and doubly so after the atrocity she'd arrived at, it was that her own death clock was in perpetual motion. She already had a ticket across the river Styx, she was simply waiting for Charon to arrive.

No, I can't think like that. Not anymore. Cindy needs me.

She shook her head, as if she could forcefully remove the intrusive, bleak thoughts from her mind. If she were going to be responsible for her young niece's future, she knew she needed to rewire her brain into believing in *her own* future. Not her inevitable death.

Detective Moore jogged to her desk, the urgency in her step pulling Laurie from her thoughts.

"Oh, Detective Moore, everything okay? You startled me," Laurie said.

"No, things aren't okay. We just received a call from a private ambulance company. There has been an accident over on Reservoir Avenue. I gotta go."

"Just like that? What about the investigation? Surely

that takes precedence over a car accident."

"Laurie, your family's case will still be worked on while we respond to other calls. We can't just put every-thing aside to work on one case. And the plate of one of the vehicles is registered to one of our own. The officer who rescued Cindy was involved and according to the caller, he's dead. And not only that, but if the caller is to be believed, the scene itself is going to be a nightmare to recreate. I've gotta get there and check this out."

"Okay, I'll grab my coat and come with you," Laurie said.

"Not this time. Let me go survey the scene, then I'll come back and take you to the hospital."

Laurie huffed but there was nothing she could do. Detective Moore wasn't going to simply change her mind, and it wasn't like Laurie had a leg to stand on. It was an active scene, of course she couldn't be there. The situa-tion nagged at the back of her mind. It was weird . . . the officer who'd saved Cindy's life lost his own just a few hours later. The world was full of odd coincidences. What else could it be? The man who'd committed the murders was dead, so it wasn't like he could have been responsible somehow. Unless there was an accomplice.

Laurie mentioned the accomplice theory to Detective Moore, who simply nodded and inferred that it wasn't likely, but obviously, they couldn't rule it out yet.

"I'll fill you in on whatever I can when I get back, then we'll go see your niece. Hang tight," Detective Moore said and jogged off, presumably to her vehicle, while Laurie took a seat, once again left to her thoughts. And her doubts.

Chapter Seven

Cindy sat up in the hospital bed, one of the newer ones that inflated and deflated in certain spots as you moved. It was comfortable, and she thought it was neat. She'd never seen a hospital bed like that before. Then again, aside from tonight, she couldn't remember a time she'd ever stayed overnight in a hospital. She remembered her sister, Katy, had been admitted after getting in a bad car wreck with her ex-boyfriend. And Mom, too, right before she passed. She thought about how horrible her mother's battle with cancer had been. She remembered thinking at the time that nothing could have been worse than what her mother had endured. But after Christmas Eve, she wasn't so sure. At least her mom hadn't been brutally murdered or tortured. Though even at her young age, Cindy realized cancer, and the treatment of it, was a certain kind of torture in its own right.

Cindy cried. She remembered the awful scene back

at the house, Sprinkles shooting Katy in the head with a gun. Blood and skull fragments spraying from her ruined head like a bursting melon.

The nurse came in, saw her crying, and gave her a big hug. "Oh, hunny, everything is gonna be okay," Liosha said. The woman swiped at the tears sliding down Cindy's cheeks.

What did this woman know? How could everything "be okay"? Just another lie adults tell children when they think the kids are too young to hear the truth. Her mother had died of cancer, and everyone else in her family was brutally murdered by the unlikely team of a lunatic in a Santa costume and her mom's Christmas elf doll—a toy that had somehow come alive. She wished she had never found that damn thing in the attic. If she had just ignored the noises maybe Dad, Adam, and Katy would still be here. They'd be opening gifts from under the tree right now, eating breakfast, watching Christmas movies, and sipping hot chocolate by the fireplace.

"Cindy, your vitals are looking good, much better than they have any right to be. This bag up here is just to keep you hydrated. I know it doesn't seem like it, but in extreme cold you can get dehydrated. This other bag is to fight off infection," Liosha said, waving her hand at the IV fluids hanging from the metal pole. "With everything that happened to you, it's very important that you don't get an infection. The doctor is going to refer you to a really good oral surgeon to see what they can do to fix up your mouth. And your foot will require more time to heal before we have a better idea of next steps. They already removed some of the dead skin so it doesn't make your foot worse, but you may need another surgery to get rid of more. Frostbite, especially on the feet, can be tricky, so it may be some time before we know for sure. Hopefully all we need to do is get rid of some more of the dead tissue from the cold. Thank God you arrived when you did."

Thank God? Cindy knew that was bullshit. God didn't exist. If that were the case, why would God allow such horrific things to happen? Cindy might be a child, but she was smart enough to realize that the concept of gods was something humans liked to tell themselves existed, nothing more.

If there was anyone to thank, it was the officer who found her. Though she wasn't thankful for him at the moment either. She would have welcomed death. The thought of the officer who saved her made her think once more about Sprinkles, about the deaths he was responsible for. And where he may be hiding.

Cindy pushed Liosha's arms away, picked up the pad, and began writing.

Where is the cop?

"Hunny, he's probably asleep right now. He must have had a long night. I can call the station and see if they can send him over so you can meet him now that you're no longer in danger."

Cindy's eyes bulged. She scribbled furiously. ***DO NOT BRING THE ELF. IT'S BAD. DO NOT LET IT COME HERE.***

"Oh, hunny, the toy isn't bad. I know it was around when bad things happened to you, but the toy isn't bad."

Cindy grunted, upset this woman was coddling her,

treating her like a child. How hard was it to listen? ***I DON'T WANT THE ELF HERE. TELL HIM TO DESTROY IT. IT IS EVIL.***

Liosha sighed, shook her head. "Okay, whatever you say. I'll call the station and as for Officer Durgin . . . if he's not there, I'll leave a message and let him know you would like to meet him. I'll even request that they leave the elf at the station. Maybe some other little boy or girl might want it. Does that work for you?"

Cindy nodded in agreement, hiding her disappointment. It *didn't* work for her. Sprinkles needed to be destroyed. Chopped into little pieces, burnt to a crisp, and scattered to the wind. But clearly this woman, who obviously meant well, wasn't going to do as she insisted. Adults were all the same. They thought they knew best. No matter how good their intentions may be, they couldn't do right by kids. Not because they were assholes, but because they simply didn't understand what it was like to be a kid anymore. And they weren't willing to admit they could be wrong, and a child could actually know best.

"So, breakfast will be here soon, and you're in the clear to have soft foods like applesauce and pudding. Do you like chocolate or vanilla?"

Cindy wasn't hungry, but she knew if she didn't eat now, she'd be hungry later, and being stuck in a hospital, she wouldn't get the luxury of eating whenever the mood struck her. She scribbled on the paper. ***Can I have applesauce and two of each pudding?***

"Yeah, sure you can," Liosha said, a smile on her face.

Outside her room, Cindy heard yelling, "I'm gonna kill you when these handcuffs come off, Smythe, you rat fuck. Just you wait. I'm gonna unscrew your head and shit down your neck. I'm gonna tear a hole in you—" There was a noise like a *hissssss*, and then the man's yelling turned into screams of pain.

What's going on out there? Cindy handed the paper to Liosha, hands trembling.

"That," Liosha said, "is a prisoner from the super-maximum security prison. I think the officer escorting him pepper sprayed him."

Cindy's nose itched and she felt a tickle in her throat. She coughed and saw Liosha rubbing her watery eyes.

"Yep, he pepper sprayed him. And if we're getting the residual of it here, he used the stuff he's not even supposed to take out inside the hospital. I'm gonna call the building and talk to his boss. God, I hate that asshole. Of all the officers that come here, he's by far the worst." She coughed again before continuing. "I'm gonna find a fan to push the fumes away from you. Hopefully there won't be any more disturbances. Why don't you put your TV on so you don't have to listen to all that racket?"

Cindy flipped through the channels, searching for something to watch even though she didn't feel like it. She kept the volume low. She'd rather listen to whatever craziness was going on in the room next door. At least that way, the sound of the TV wouldn't drown out noises in her own room.

Little things moved quietly, and Cindy was petrified of what might lurk in the dark.

Walter Smythe stood in the hallway coughing, snot running down his nose. He'd gotten a bit too liberal with the pepper spray. But what was he supposed to do? Filmore had it coming. It seemed like twice a week this guy was pulling some stunt or other to get sent on a trip to the ER, resulting in a loss of thousands of dollars of taxpayers' money. And the man had threatened him! Who's to say he wouldn't have taken his frustrations out on the nursing staff? It wouldn't be the first time. So yeah, maybe he had been proactive with the spray, but Smythe figured it was better to be proactive than reactive when it came to safety and security.

Unfortunately, department policy did not back him up on that call. He'd have to talk with the nurses, get a feel for what they'd seen or heard. Then he could figure out how he'd type up the use of force report. Hopefully there weren't any witnesses because it was much easier to paper fuck a prisoner when there were no conflicting reports, be they from within the department or some other agency. Even a civilian witness could be made to have their credibility questioned. Still, he was a little worried. It was bad enough that he'd smashed the man in the face earlier. Hopefully the driver and his little freak girlfriend would keep their mouths shut.

Smythe knew he needed to chill out, knew internal affairs had their eyes on him. He was part of the old guard, having been around for twenty years. The days of teeing off on an inmate with no repercussions were long gone. The world called for kinder, gentler corrections. He thought maybe he should retire, cash out his pension before he lost his job, or worse, ended up with a conviction for assault.

Back in the room, Officer Smythe unloaded the gear and set everything up while waiting for his partner to make his way to the room. It would probably be a while. Hospital posts were a two-man job, but when an ambulance was required, one officer rode in the back and the other drove the car. That meant Rogers—his partner—didn't have anyone to stop him from flirting with the nurses as he made his way through the massive building. If Smythe knew anything about his partner, he knew this: since it had taken the man this long to get from the car to the room, then flirting was probably the least of what was going on. He didn't know how the man did it, but somehow, he had four different nurse notches in his belt. He collected their panties the way the Predator collected spines. Rumor amongst coworkers was that Rogers had a Maglite in his pants for a pecker. Obviously that helped drop the scrubs. Smythe wouldn't know; his ex-girlfriend had rudely joked with him that he could use a thimble for a jockstrap.

Smythe watched the nurse assigned to Filmore as she flushed his eyes with water and baby shampoo, trying to clear the chemical from the man's eyes. He'd really gotten the fucker good. Maybe he'd keep his mouth shut next time.

Finished, the nurse turned around, startling Smythe.

She'd caught him staring at her ass. He smiled at her, and she laughed. "Not in your wildest dreams, loser," she said before walking out the door. He ground his teeth, looking at the name on the whiteboard. "Liosha, huh? Maybe I'll teach you and that big dumper a lesson," he said.

Chapter Eight

Detective Moore arrived at the scene of the accident frustrated and pissed off. While the worst of the storm was over, snow continued to fall and travel remained at a snail's pace. The department was kitted out with top-of-the-line SUVs, but at the end of the day, Mother Nature always trumped the technological advancements of man. She was at the mercy of the roads. At least most of the citizens of Glenwood had taken the state of emergency declaration to heart and kept their vehicles off the damn streets. In years past, that was a major problem for the city when they had snowstorms. But this nor'easter had been different, and for once in their damned lives, it seemed as if everyone had actually agreed that it would be better to stay home than to risk the drive.

Aside from this asshole trucker, anyway.

Jennifer opened the driver's side door, stepped out of the department SUV. She shook her head. Fucking Officer Durgin. He was a good cop and a good man who'd been on the way home from work after what had to have been an awful night, considering he was the first on the scene at the Feltcher murders. Then he'd stayed well past the end of his shift making sure the paperwork was completed and filed correctly. No shortcuts, no bullshit.

Arriving on the scene of the accident, at first glance, it appeared as if Durgin was somehow at fault. Though it had to be said, if the trucker had heeded the state of emergency declaration, it wouldn't have mattered if Durgin had entered the wrong lane, for whatever reason. You can't hit an oncoming vehicle that isn't there. She cursed the other driver's stupidity.

But what happened here? Did Officer Durgin nod off, a result of the long shift? Jennifer hoped not. There were no case studies about how often off-the-job accidents occurred due to a lack of rest among law enforcement officers, but Jennifer wasn't stupid. Anyone with a semi-functional brain could tell you a lack of quality rest caused accidents all the time. She herself had worked plenty of long, shitty hours for the department. She knew what it was like to drive home after a sixteen-hour shift. How many times had she almost done exactly what it appeared Durgin had done?

In their line of work, you were prepared to lose coworkers. It did nothing to ease the pain of loss, but you showed up daily with the knowledge tucked in the back of your mind that either you, or one of your peers, might not make it home. Deaths like Durgin's, though, outside the line of duty? Those were far tougher to deal with. It made you question how you could put your life on the line day in and day out, come home safe and sound, but still have your time card punched in the blink of an eye.

She approached the scene, and as reported, a humongous, bright red snowblower sat ridiculously out of place. Had she ever seen a snowblower this large before? Maybe an industrial-sized one, surely not residential. Nothing someone would use on their driveway, that was for damn sure.

She took notes, made observations, and when a patrol car finally arrived, she delegated the remainder of the menial tasks to them. With the crime scene out of the way, a coworker's death weighing heavily on her shoulders, and more questions than answers, she set off for Glenwood Memorial Hospital. No doubt the EMTs would have nothing fruitful to contribute to the investigation but it was part of the job, and Detective Jennifer Moore was nothing if not thorough.

Chapter Nine

Laurie drummed her fingers on the desk, watching the film of milk float around the surface of her lukewarm coffee. She was on her fourth cup, and though she was tired and wanted more caffeine, the coffee at the station was atrocious. One more cup and she might puke on Detective Moore's desk.

She looked at the clock. Detective Moore—Jennifer—had been gone for an hour already. How far was the scene of the accident? And how far was the hospital? It was still morning but surely the hospital had squared away its power issue. How long could they reasonably operate on a generator? And not only that, even if they were still on a generator, someone at the hospital had to have a fucking heart, right? Laurie knew they had policies and procedures to follow, but surely *someone* could over-rule the policy in favor of doing the right thing. Were they really going to let a poor child sit in the hospital on Christmas morning, by herself, the day after her entire family had been murdered?

Laurie didn't think even the most jaded member of the hospital's staff could be so cruel, so heartless. The thought of Cindy sitting there all alone got her blood pumping.

Fuck this, she thought. *I don't give a damn about their state of emergency. I'm not a suspect, I'm not being detained, and I'm not waiting here one more fucking minute.* She pushed back from the desk, the chair scraping the floor as she rose to her feet. Laurie felt everyone's eyes on her, but she ignored the stares. She tossed her coat on and marched out the front door. She was thankful Detective Moore had ordered an officer to drive her rental to the station, otherwise she would be trapped. But now, as she sat in the driver's seat, she couldn't help but feel optimistic about the future. Things would be rough going forward, but they were family, and family stuck by each other. Laurie knew that now.

Chapter Ten

At last, the snow had let up. The brutal nor'easter had relinquished its stranglehold on the town of Glenwood. The snow was hardly falling at this point, and soon the plows would be able to make good headway on the roads. At the state level, the highways were already well on their way to being fully operational.

Anthony scrolled through his phone mindlessly, hopping from one social media app to the next. Instagram, TikTok, Facebook, Snapchat, YouTube . . . he had them all and he was addicted to the dopamine rush he got with each like, comment, follow, and subscription. Though in the early stages, Anthony Ramsdell hoped to grow his various pages with a steady stream of content. He'd been playing accordion since he was a child and was quite good at it. It pained him to see other players—players he had known from the scene and had considered to be less skilled than himself—making enough money to not only make a living comfortably but also travel the world playing the accordion.

He knew it was jealousy, and he hated feeling that way, but he just couldn't help it. It should have been him blowing up on YouTube. He should be the one making albums and touring the world. He'd been better than the other guys. But his father had taken ill and both his brother and sister refused to help, so Anthony had made the hard decision to give up on his dream. It pained him to do so, and he knew his father felt the same way, probably even worse.

When Anthony was a young boy, it had been his father, Anthony Sr., who had set him on the path. He didn't have to imagine how his father felt, being the reason Anthony gave up his dream, the man didn't let a day go by without an apology. "I'm sorry I ruined things for you. Please, don't give up on our dream. I've lived long enough. I want to see you happy again," he'd say, tears streaming down his gaunt face.

In the end, his father's condition had deteriorated so badly that the man was barely aware of his surroundings and communication was all but impossible. But on the last day, he had a moment of lucidity. It was like someone flipped a light switch in his brain. Suddenly, his speech was coherent. The vacancy in his eyes vanished, replaced with the awareness of his younger, healthier self.

His time was up, and both father and son knew it. Anthony Sr. had looked his son directly in the eyes, beckoned him closer. "It's not too late," he'd said, his throat raspy from months of minimal use. "I know you can do it. Please, Anthony. Do it for yourself. Do it for me."

Anthony Sr. closed his eyes at that moment and never opened them again. He hadn't passed immediately, he'd lived another day or so, but that had been the final moment Anthony shared with his father.

He tapped away at the screen, scheduling a video to upload simultaneously on various platforms. The song was a fun one, not the usual classics accordion players cover on their channels. He liked to show range, mix things up a bit. And, truth be told, it helped to draw in a larger audience that normally wouldn't give a damn about some guy playing the accordion. Some people loved Frank Sinatra; others loved to hear pop music covers. Why not attract both crowds? With the video ready to go, he switched over to his *personal* account. He liked to keep the music stuff separate from the other stuff. To give himself some privacy and to keep the algorithm from getting confused.

Every few swipes there was a clip, some woman being interviewed in the street after a night of drinking. He swiped, and there it was again, the Southern drawl burned into his brain forever. *Aww, you gotta give 'em that hawk tua, spit on that thang!*

In the seat next to him, Kendra laughed. "You like that?" she asked, putting her phone aside and leaning closer to Anthony. "Show me why they call you *Tony Cannoli.*"

Anthony burst out laughing, unable to contain himself at the sheer absurdity of using his stage name as sexual innuendo. Kendra laughed, then quickly gave him a death stare. Anthony stopped laughing, the urge to bust a nut overriding the urge to laugh.

"Good choice," she said, unzipping his pants.

She leaned over his penis, a long stream of saliva dangled from her mouth before landing on the head. She stroked his shaft, the saliva acting as lube while her hand slid up and down. He closed his eyes and tilted his head back.

"Fuck," he moaned.

"Get in the back," she said, letting go of his penis.

Anthony didn't need to be told twice. He hopped in the back, pants and underwear dangling under his ass. He lay back on the stretcher and Kendra took her place between his legs but didn't make a move to touch him.

Anthony sat up. "Swallow my tube steak, baby," he said.

This time, Kendra couldn't help but laugh. "Did you just call your dick a tube steak?"

Anthony's cheeks turned red. "I was just trying to be funny since you called my dick a cannoli."

"True. Lay down and let's do this. I've been so fucking horny since that eighteen-wheeler, and it's time we do something other than teasing."

Kendra tied her hair back and leaned forward. Anthony gasped as her lips pushed past his glans. She bobbed her head up and down, while at the same time stroking his shaft. Anthony groaned and almost popped when she started turning her wrist while she was stroking it. He knew he was in for some good sex. Any woman who did the wrist turn knew what she was doing, and he was damn glad to be on the receiving end of this tonight. He gripped the sides of the stretcher and grunted.

"Not yet, handsome," she said as she slid her pants down.

Anthony propped up on his elbows and watched Kendra disrobe. He saw her vagina glistening and started stroking his cock. "Sit on this dick, baby."

"Not until you eat my pussy. I know you're already close, and I'm gonna get my orgasm either way. So you can eat me now, or you're gonna do it after you finish. Which do you prefer?"

His lip curled in disgust, and he hopped off the stretcher, squeezing between the storage containers of supplies and the stretcher. Was she serious? Kendra must have seen the look on his face, read his mind, because she grinned, kicked her pants free from her ankles, and took his place on the stretcher, opening her legs wide.

He bit his lip. His cock felt like it was going to burst. He knelt in front of the stretcher and began kissing her thighs, licking the area around her vagina. He massaged around it, stroking with his hands and tongue, always in the direction of her sex but not yet touching it. This time, it was Kendra that moaned and before Anthony knew it, her fingers gripped his hair and she shoved his face forward. He ran his tongue in circles while using two fingers inside her, flexing them in a "come here" motion. It didn't take long before he found the rhythm and spots she liked best. If you paid attention to a woman's body, it wasn't rocket science. Besides, Anthony thought of it like the Jonah Hill quote from *Superbad*: "Some women pride themselves on their dick taking abilities." And he thought that was true, but Anthony took pride in his pussy eating abilities. He liked to tell himself that any guy could pump away, but the *real way* to make sure a woman you slept with would come back for more was to eat her so good she'd never forget you.

He felt her thighs squeezing his head harder. He strained his eyes to look up but they couldn't see past his new flesh earmuffs. But he could taste her, and though her cries were muffled because of the way she'd gripped his head with her legs, he could still hear her crying out as she came, feeling her body rocking in waves. He kept going, attacking her clit with renewed vigor until she pushed his head away and told him to stop.

He smiled, couldn't help it. Anthony wasn't exactly bedding every woman he wanted, but his ego loved it every time he made a woman finish. He absentmindedly stroked his penis while Kendra turned over. He grabbed her calves and pulled her closer. Kendra slid off the stretcher. He used his knees to slide her legs apart, grabbed her by the ponytail with his right hand, and with his left hand pushed between her shoulder blades. She was standing, bent over the stretcher, her head held up from Anthony pulling her hair.

He parted her lips with the tip of his penis and she groaned. Fumbling around in her hair, Anthony got a better grip, closer to the base of the skull, and began pounding away.

They humped, sweaty in the van despite the frigid temperatures outside the vehicle.

The rear door opened and quietly clicked closed behind the pair.

Anthony felt something graze his leg while he was giving Kendra everything he had, sweat dripping profusely, his shirt collar damp around his neck.

In the front of the vehicle, the radio turned on. Mariah Carey poured out her soul to the one person she wanted for Christmas, but the rutting couple was too lost in their lust to hear her.

Next to them, a small hand turned some dials and switches, clicking a machine to life. Anthony squeezed his eyes tighter, trying to force Kendra's warm body out of his mind and think of anything else to hold back his impending orgasm.

He pulled out, willed his climax away. Soon he would finish, but he wanted a few more minutes of fun before that happened. "You get on top," he said.

The toy elf, still unseen, crawled underneath the stretcher.

Kendra stood up and ripped her sweaty shirt off while Anthony lay back on the stretcher. Propped up on his elbows, he watched her move closer, watched her breasts sway as she maneuvered into position, straddling him.

Anthony arched his hips to meet her warmth as it dropped down over his cock. He grabbed her breasts, squeezed, and tweaked her nipples. She rocked back and forth, grinding their genitals together, and he grabbed her hips.

His gaze remained on her boobs; he couldn't help it. They might be the best breasts he'd seen in real life. "Your tits are fucking just . . . so juicy, dude," he said, reaching up for her chest once more. "These would win in a fucking titty contest!"

She grinned and shook her head but kept fucking without missing a beat. He'd been trying to make her laugh, resorting to movie quotes to further delay blowing his load, but he was getting ready to pop and no amount of distraction could stop the imminent eruption.

"*Hehehe.*" Anthony heard someone giggle before a voice shouted, "*Clear!*"

Sprinkles popped up behind Kendra and smashed defibrillator paddles on either side of her head. Her body shook uncontrollably. "Unnnnghhhhhh," she groaned, as the electricity jolted through her and Anthony's warm cum shot inside her.

The volts passed through to Anthony's body, shocking him to a lesser extent. He opened his eyes to the sight of Kendra's smoking skull, hair ablaze as her body violently jerked. A large toy elf stood on the stretcher behind her holding defibrillator paddles to her head, laughing hysterically.

"*Doctor Sprinkles is here, everyone get clear!*" the elf shouted as he continued shocking Kendra. He let go of the paddles and her body slumped to the side, hair still on fire, burst eyeballs oozing from their sockets.

Anthony couldn't believe his eyes. He'd lost his mind, had to have. The gruesome scene from earlier had caused him to snap. "You're not real," Anthony said, trying to convince himself he'd had a lapse in reality.

"*Oh, I'm real, all right,*" Sprinkles said. "*And you're gonna pay for throwing that coffee in my face, you naughty, naughty boy.*" Sprinkles snapped his fingers and a large, sharp candy cane appeared in the palm of his hand. He rammed it in a downward arc, driving the needlelike tip through the base of Anthony's penis and impaling his gonads, pinning him to the stretcher by his nuts.

"Looks like I've got you by the balls, don't I, Tony Cannoli?" Sprinkles laughed.

Anthony screamed, looking down at his ruined ball bag. Blood pooled around the wound and he vomited, the pain too much to handle. He watched, only half aware as the giggling, demented elf slowly crawled across the stretcher on all four of his small toy limbs. The elf stopped at his groin, grinned. *"Let's see what's in* this *sack!"* the elf said gleefully.

Anthony screamed in agony as the doll worked its fingers into the hole in his scrotum and ripped it wider. He tried to get away but he was lanced by the testicles to the stretcher, and each time he pushed away, the shock-wave of pain threatened to send him into the void of unconsciousness. The vacant look in the murderous toy's eyes as it ripped his sack open spurred Anthony into action. He didn't want to do it, but he had no choice, so he dug in with his palms and heels, pushing himself backward. The tear grew wider, the sound of skin splitting drowned out by his guttural screams.

"Ohhh, watch that vein in your head, buddy. It looks like it's gonna burst!" Sprinkles giggled.

With one last push, Anthony tore free from the candy cane, spilling into the space between the two front seats. A trail of blood led from the stretcher to where he had fallen, legs folded over his shoulders. Blood gushed from his ruined scrotum, saturating his navy blue polo uniform top. The pain was crippling, and Anthony did his best to get up, but he moved like molasses. He tried the door handle but it was locked. Anthony tried to unlock it, but with a snap of the elf's fingers, a whirlwind of ice crystals froze the handle and locking mechanism solid. He pulled his hand back, the frozen door handle burning cold.

"You're not going anywhere," Sprinkles said as he lifted the candy cane to his mouth. Anthony's newly removed testicle was stuck to the sharp tip like a piece of steak on a kebab skewer. The living doll placed the nut in his mouth and chewed.

Anthony sobbed. There was nowhere to go. Kendra was dead and he was stuck in the vehicle with a murderous toy who'd just eaten one of his family jewels. He wished he was dead and knew it wouldn't be long before his wish came true. With luck, it would be quick and painless. There was so much he still wanted to do, and though his life wasn't flashing before his eyes, he did wish that he'd gotten to achieve the dream he shared with his father. Now they'd both go to the grave knowing he'd never made it.

Sprinkles spat globs of the chewed-up testicle at Anthony. *"Stringy,"* he said. *"And eat some fucking pineapple, for Christ's sake. Imagine if poor Kendra had swallowed your sour seed. It's bitter. Disgusting! You try a piece."*

With short, quick steps, Sprinkles closed the gap between them and placed the candy cane to Anthony's lips. He clamped his mouth shut. No way, he wasn't going to eat his own nut. He'd rather die.

"Okay, lover boy. You don't want to eat your nut, silly me. I wouldn't want to eat mine either." Sprinkles wrinkled his eyes, frowned. *"But I feel bad that I didn't let you and your little naughty friend finish. And I gotta be honest —because Santa doesn't like liars—you two sickos made me feel a little naughty."* Sprinkles undid his leather belt, the golden buckle clanking against the side of the stretcher. The doll removed its tunic and dropped it onto the floor, exposing a large, plastic penis.

Anthony shook his head. How was this possible? What the hell was going on? He kept trying the frozen door handle as the elf chuckled maniacally, its erect dick bobbing and swaying with his laughter. Anthony was woozy from the loss of blood, but the cold embrace of death couldn't come fast enough. He watched in horror as Sprinkles snapped his fingers again and a stream of ice crystals swirled furiously around the toy cock, shrouding it. When the crystals dissipated, Anthony screamed.

Gone was the plastic penis, replaced by a giant, phallic candy cane. The red and white striped cock was shaped like a normal, circumcised dick, except the head ended in a sharpened point. Sprinkles stroked his deadly peppermint pecker. *"She sucked your candy cane, Tony Cannoli. Won't you suck on mine?"* Sprinkles laughed, his voice grating. The mocking way he said his stage name just felt disgusting to Anthony.

The living doll snapped his fingers and two more streams of ice crystals shot forward, freezing Anthony's hands to the door and the dashboard, trapping him in place. He screamed as Sprinkles came closer.

"*Open wide,*" the doll said, grinning. "*This is one girthy candy cane.*"

Anthony clamped his mouth shut and Sprinkles grabbed him by the hair, thrusting his hips forward. The sharp tip of the candy cane cock parted Anthony's lips, shattering his front teeth. Blood gushed from the wound and Anthony, screaming, choked on the broken bits of teeth that had fallen into his throat. As Sprinkles penetrated further, Anthony's screams became muffled, the candy cane taking up all the space in his mouth.

Sprinkles grunted and kept thrusting, in and out, the sharp tip of his candy cane lightly piercing the back of Anthony's throat.

"*Ugghhh, I'm gonna finish, Tony, take it all,*" Sprinkles said with one last deep thrust. The sharp head of the candy cane penis punched a hole through Anthony's pharynx and shattered the cervical portion of his spinal column. Blood poured out of his mouth as the body convulsed. The elf took a step back, letting go of Anthony, whose body crumpled to the floor of the vehicle. Sprinkles' penis reverted from a phallic candy cane weapon back to a plastic penis before finally becoming a formless patch of flat plastic.

Blood and peppermint ejaculate oozed down the black door paneling.

"*Now that head was to die for, right, Tony Cannoli?*" Sprinkles asked, his voice high-pitched and terrifyingly musical.

Sprinkles snapped his fingers and was once more

fully dressed. The ice on the door handle and lock melted away.

With another snap, Santa's bag appeared. The doll crawled inside, rummaging around before reappearing with a long knife, its edges serrated. Sprinkles grabbed Kendra's fried and frizzled hair and began sawing away at the neck of her corpse.

Chapter Eleven

Liosha stood in the corner of the room, letting the doctor talk to Cindy. Her prognosis was good, and though she was a hot mess, Liosha thought she was holding up much better than they had any right to expect, given the circumstances. The little girl was one tough cookie, that's for sure. It made her sad thinking about it. What would a child have to go through in her life to be able to withstand the type of loss she'd endured last night?

The doctor left the room and Liosha went to Cindy. "You're gonna be okay, little one. You're going to have to come back for more tests later to make sure your foot is good, but the doctor thinks it will be fine eventually." She rubbed Cindy's back, the girl smiled.

Cindy reached for her pad and scribbled. **When is the next nurse going to be here? I don't want you to leave.**

The note brought an ear-to-ear grin to Liosha's face. Some patients you couldn't wait to get away from, but not Cindy. She was the type of patient you looked forward to each day. A good girl, a fighter. You couldn't help but root for her and want to be a part of her recovery process. "So, I've got good news and bad news. The good news, I'll be your nurse for at least the next shift. A lot of the staff couldn't make it in today because of the storm and the state of emergency, so they asked everyone who was already here to stay and work overtime. Now here's the bad news. It's busier here during the day. Even if we don't have many new patients coming in today, there is just more that is done during the day, and with us being short-staffed, it means we're all going to have to do more work. So yes, I will be here today, sweet girl, but it might take me longer to get to you. If I'm slow to come by, don't get upset. I'll be here, I'm just super busy. There's a chance they may continue diverting patients to the other area hospitals; if that happens, I'll be more available."

Cindy scribbled on the pad again. ***Okay, I'll try not to bother you too much. Just don't forget about me!***

"How could anybody forget you? You're precious. Food should be here any minute. It's actually a bit late, so hopefully it won't be much longer. I've gotta go to the nurses' station but I'll be back. I'll see what kind of books we have lying around the hospital for when I come around. Why don't you watch some TV?"

Cindy nodded and started flipping through the stations.

Just as Liosha made it back to the nurses' station, an alarm sounded for one of the rooms at the other end of the hall. She dropped what she was doing and ran to the patient emergency.

The day was sure to be a long one.

Chapter Twelve

Keith Filmore lay on the hospital bed, his face both throbbing from his shattered nose and burning from the pepper spray even though he'd had his face washed by hospital staff. He coughed, the irritant still doing its job, and doing it well. The nurse, a take-no-bullshit woman with perhaps the finest ass he'd ever seen in his life, had decontaminated him using cold water and baby shampoo. The worst of the burn was gone, but at random times, the harsh chemical would reactivate and he'd be in a world of hurt all over again.

The nose . . . well, he'd just have to deal with that. Miss Booty had given him pain meds to combat the damage done by that rotten fucker, Officer Smythe, but Keith hadn't taken them. He'd kept them tucked away in his mouth until he was sure Smythe's attention was elsewhere and then hidden them under the mattress. As it turned out, Filmore wasn't the only person in the room who couldn't peel his eyes from the tank she was hiding in her scrubs. If everything went according to plan, Keith would be sure to pay her a special visit, give her a little thank you for making his escape possible.

An alarm cut through the silence, startling him. A woman's voice over the intercom announced some sort of patient code, though he didn't know what the hell they meant. He assumed it had to be something serious because the few members of the staff on the floor could all be heard sprinting down the hallway.

Keith looked around, tried to see what he could, which admittedly wasn't much. He was, after all, chained to a bed by his ankle. The second corrections officer still hadn't shown up, and he knew Smythe was pissed off because he'd heard the man yelling at his watch, telling his partner to put his dick away and get back to work.

Keith also knew when the man was MIA, he was usually MIA for a long time. He'd been on enough of these hospital furloughs to know that Officer Rogers spent much of his time flirting with, and fucking, the nurses. He knew Smythe hated it because he was left without a partner guarding men like Keith. But he also knew how jealous it made Smythe. He knew a pervert when he saw one, and there was no doubt in his mind that the only difference between a rapist behind bars and someone like Smythe was that a guy like Smythe had been lucky enough to never have been arrested yet. Maybe he hadn't committed the crime. Maybe he had and nobody had come forward. Either way, with guys like Smythe, it was just a matter of time.

But right now, for Keith, it was time. With Rogers gone, Smythe distracted, and the hospital staff reacting to whatever emergency they had going on down the hall, this was his shot.

Keith ran his tongue along the space between two of his molars, pressing hard and fast until the sliver of the casing he'd peeled off a AA battery popped free. He let it fall from his mouth into his hand, keeping an eye on Smythe, who was rubbernecking the code from the doorway. *Still distracted, good,* he thought, working the battery casing into the top of the leg shackle that secured him to the bed. It would work, he knew, as long as the sliver was deep enough. He pushed further until the sliver of battery covered the small notches of the shackle completely. When he pushed it in as far as it would go, Keith closed his eyes and prayed to a god. Any god, it didn't matter to him who answered the prayer.

He pulled his foot up, keeping the sliver of battery pushed down as far as it would go, the single strand bar slid over the obstruction, the teeth not able to catch because of the battery casing. The bar opened and he was free!

Officer Smythe, still distracted in the doorway, scratched his ass, brought his hand to his nose, and sniffed.

Keith shook his head in disgust. *These guys say we're the animals. Nasty fucker.*

He placed the shackle on the mattress, holding it in his hands like a churchgoer ready to receive the body of Christ, and slid off the bed, his feet hitting the floor. To his own ears, the soft plop was gunshot loud, though in reality, nobody could have heard it. Still, Keith knew damn well people seemed to have a sixth sense when they were being snuck up on, so he crept quickly and quietly, not hesitating as he wrapped his arms around Smythe's head and neck in a rear naked choke. He dropped onto his back, wrapped his legs around Smythe's midsection, and squeezed, hoping against hope that not only had he taken the man completely by surprise, but that he would be clueless as to how to defend the attack.

The door to the room shut, the latch clicking as it caught. At first, Smythe resisted, throwing himself about like an animal caught in a trap, expending energy while mounting a defense that was ineffective. By the time Smythe stopped flailing and began trying to work out of the hold, Keith knew it was too late. He could feel the man's strength waning and he had the choke locked in deep.

It wouldn't do to have Smythe waking up, so when the man stopped trying to pry Keith's arms from his neck, he held the hold for a few more minutes until he was sure he had choked the life from the piece of shit.

Keith's heart was pounding in his chest. Sweat saturated his hospital gown, making it cling to his torso. He peeled it off his slick, shiny skin and tossed it in the corner of the room before grabbing Smythe by the ankles and dragging him into the bathroom, stripping his uniform off, then donning it himself. It was a tight fit but good enough to fool anyone who didn't look too closely.

Keith clipped the duty belt around his waist, pulled the Department of Corrections baseball cap low on his head, and slipped into the hallway.

Chapter Thirteen

arry Paul's feet were up on the desk while he reclined in the black leather office chair. His ball cap pulled low, Oakley sunglasses over his eyes despite being indoors. Normally when he worked a double at the hospital, he slept during the graveyard shift —nobody cared—but during the day, he'd be wide awake and alert, as was expected of him. But not today. Today, the security company he worked for had broken the bad news to him at the last minute. He wouldn't be going home until later in the evening. His relief had been unable to safely make it to work due to the storm, so Larry was expected to cover the shift or be fired. That was fine by him, he could use the extra money, but if they thought he was going to be forced over during the holiday season and expected the best out of him, they had another thing coming. He'd be there all day, but he wasn't going to lift a finger, and he'd be paid time and a half to do jack shit. And if they didn't like it? Well then maybe they should have given his relief the same ultimatum they gave him.

He knew he shouldn't complain. Things could be far worse. And given the situation, the morning had actually been surprisingly quiet. Larry had expected to be hammered with all manner of patients due to the storm, but the hospital had lost power and much of the staff was unable to make it to work, so they'd put out a call for all ambulances to reroute to the state's other hospitals, which apparently weren't facing the same hardships as Glenwood Memorial. Aside from the prisoner that had been transported, the only other patient to come in had been a little girl. Larry wasn't sure what had happened but from what he saw of the girl on the stretcher, someone had done a real number on her. Sick fucks littered the country these days. Who could do that to a little girl? And on Christmas, of all days.

Speaking of Glenwood Memorial, the place was a ticking time bomb, an accident waiting to happen. The building was old, and the working conditions sucked for employees, which was why even on a good day they were understaffed. Most citizens in the area with the credentials to work in a hospital chose to work elsewhere. Better pay and better conditions were a good incentive. Most of the staff at Glenwood were there either because they were in the twilight years of their careers and had worked there forever, or they lived close by and didn't want to travel. Not that travel to the other hospitals was too great a distance. The people of Rhode Island were just notorious complainers when it came to traveling. Larry recalled a buddy once telling him he'd rather drag his scrotum across a mile of broken glass than commute fifteen miles to work.

And if Larry was being honest with himself, that was exactly why he stayed put and dealt with the shit conditions. As it was, he didn't want to drive five minutes down the road to get to work, never mind a 45-minute commute through traffic. Nope, Larry would forego higher pay for time and convenience.

His eyelids fluttered and just as he was about to doze off again, a noise—a jingling bell of some sort—startled him, almost knocking him off his chair.

"The fuck was that?" he grumbled, setting the chair right and getting up from his post. Larry peeked through the one-way window in the front of his station. Nothing stood out as needing his attention, so he made to sit at his desk again but stopped short when he heard another noise. If not for the complete and utter silence, he wouldn't have been able to pick out the creepy laughter or turned around to investigate, his heart hammering in his chest.

Larry opened the door to his small station and peeked his head around the corner. He didn't know why the laughter creeped him out so much, but now, peeking out into the ghost town which served as the hospital's main entrance and lobby, his sphincter tightened and he could feel beads of sweat dripping down his arms. The perspiration tickled but there was nothing funny about the feeling in the pit of his stomach.

"Hello?" Larry called out. His voice echoed across

the room. *You'd think the fucking check-in nurse would respond,* he thought. But would she? Maybe. Or maybe not. He wasn't on the best of terms with the female staff members. He had a tendency to shoot his shot with any woman who so much as glanced in his direction, and so far, he was batting 0 for 10 in that regard. He didn't get it. He thought he was nice-looking enough, thought he had a good personality and a great sense of humor. But for some reason, they wouldn't give him the time of day and he resented them for it. So no, thinking about it a little more, it would have been just like those stuck-up bitches to ignore him. They'd get their jollies by blowing him off for no other reason than they knew ignoring him would go straight up his ass.

Frustrated with the lack of attention he felt he deserved, Larry pushed aside the heebie-jeebies and marched straight toward the check-in desk. Lucy was on duty, but from what he could tell, she wasn't at her station. In fact, nobody seemed to be there. As he drew closer, he heard the laughing once more, much louder this time. It seemed to be coming from behind the check-in area. What the fuck was so funny? He picked up the pace, ready to fling the door open and give Lucy a piece of his mind, really give her something to laugh about. He scanned his credentials card, the door beeped and he threw it open so hard it slammed against the wall.

"What the fuck is everyone's problem . . . " he trailed off, frozen by the impossible sight before him.

In the middle of the staff portion of the check-in area was a blue and red, child-sized indoor trampoline. The severed heads of the reception area staff members bounced up and down with each leap made by the imp dressed as an elf jumping on it. It was a hideous, moon-gray thing wearing a green tunic, the bells on its costume jingling as it danced around the trampoline gleefully, giggling and laughing. It was covered in blood and gore, as was the reception area. It seemed to cover every surface. The four heads bounced around until they fell off the side of the trampoline. One of them, Lucy's, rolled along the floor and stopped when it collided with the pile of bodies that belonged to the severed heads.

Larry backpedaled but before he reached the door, the elf turned to him, snapped his fingers, and the door slammed shut behind him. He tried pulling the handle down but it was locked. With shaky hands, Larry fumbled with his credentials card until, at last, he managed to scan it. The lock beeped but flashed red and the door handle still wouldn't budge. He tried the mechanism again and the result was the same.

Larry heard the jingling of the bells grow louder and he looked back, his eyes wide with disbelief. The elf was drawing nearer. What the fuck kind of sick nightmare was he stuck in? Real or nightmare, Larry didn't know, but either way, he wasn't ready to die, not even in his dreams. He looked around the nurses' station for something, anything, he could use to knock the little son of a bitch into next week. Off to his left, he spotted a mop sticking out of a large yellow bucket. Larry ran to it, his sneakers squeaking on the floor as he snatched the wooden handle and brandished it like a baseball bat, the dirty blue threads of the mophead awkwardly falling over his shoulder. It smelled disgusting and he was skeeved out, but the dirty mop was the only thing within reach.

"C'mon, you little bitch," he said. "You kill a bunch of women and think you're hot shit, but I'll knock your stupid little head off your goddamn shoulders, you overgrown, plastic piece of shit." The tremor in his voice betrayed his false bravado.

"I'm not a piece of shit young man, I'm Sprinkles!" the elf said gleefully as it snapped its fingers and a taser materialized in its hand from a swirling cloud of frost.

"What the hell are you?"

"Silly, Larry, I told you already. I'm Sprinkles. Maybe you shouldn't be such a misogynist, Larry. The women you call bitches put up a better fight than you, sissy boy. And they don't wet the bed. But you do, right? You steal your mommy's panties and play with your little ding-a-ling and wet your bed like a little baby."

"Shut the fuck up!" Larry shouted as he swung the mop like a Louisville Slugger, torquing his entire body.

But Sprinkles was deceptively fast, ducking the arc with ease. The force of the swing knocked the security guard off balance, and he slipped on the floor.

Larry scrambled to his knees and jabbed the wooden handle at the elf, but Sprinkles beat him to the punch again, hopping out of range of the makeshift weapon.

In the blink of an eye, Sprinkles fired the taser, both probes shooting forward and embedding in Larry's crotch. He dropped to the ground and convulsed as the weapon jolted his body via his nut sack.

With Larry incapacitated, Sprinkles dropped his trousers, exposing his rock-hard candy cane penis. The malevolent elf snapped his fingers and more of the magical ice crystals swirled around his body before disappearing up his rectum. Sprinkles stood ramrod straight, wincing as if in pain. "*Ugghhhh, it hurts,*" the elf said before he reached one hand around his backside, plunging it inside his plastic rectal cavity.

The elf giggled. "*How did this fit up there? Santa really went to town on my ass!*"

Slowly, making a show out of it, the elf pulled a Louisville Slugger wrapped with barbed wire from his ass.

Larry, in pain and now aware of the elf's barbaric butt plug, screamed and tried to scramble to his feet, but Sprinkles hopped forward and swung the bat in an overhead arc, crashing down with a force that should have been impossible for a thing his size.

Larry crumpled, the pain a fire at the top of his head. His vision blurred and his thoughts swam. The back of his skull felt wet all the way to the base of his neck, which he thought was odd because he hadn't been outside in the snow recently. He tried to wipe the moistness away, but his arms were too heavy to move.

He thought he heard something, giggling maybe. Children's laughter. But then the fog in his brain dissipated. His vision cleared in time to see the elf raise the bat again before bringing it down once more on Larry's skull. The pain wasn't so bad this time, then everything went dark and Larry knew nothing else.

Sprinkles continued gleefully tittering. The bat rising and falling. The first few impacts were announced by loud, heavy thunking sounds. But soon the cracks gave way to wet squelching noises. Tattered pieces of flesh flew through the air, ribbons of skin stuck to the bat. Each swing spraying blood across the nurses' station until Larry's entire upper torso looked like a pile of raw hamburger.

Chapter Fourteen

Detective Moore cruised the streets as fast as she dared. The roads were still bad and would be for quite some time, but she wanted to get a statement from the EMTs who had called it in. One of their own was dead, and frankly, despite Durgin being obviously dead from a car accident, the rest of the scene made absolutely no sense. She couldn't fathom how a snowblower like the one at the crime scene—because that's what it was now—would have ended up *at* the scene, never mind how it ended up as a tool of murder.

Who had operated it? Who was the victim? How had the man ended up inside the machine? Had Durgin stumbled upon the scene and hit the truck? Or had the murder occurred after the accident had taken place? She knew she wasn't going to get the answers she needed from the EMTs, but she needed to do her due diligence and speak to everyone she could, gather the facts, and take her investigation from there.

Clipped to a cup holster, Detective Moore's phone

"

buzzed. The notification on her dash popped up, indicating it was the station calling. She pressed the green phone icon on the console's screen. "Detective Moore," she answered.

The voice on the other line said, "Detective, sorry to bother you, but that woman you left at your desk—"

"What about her?" Moore interrupted, a hint of frustration in her voice. "I'm kinda busy here and the roads are shit. We already had one officer die in this mess and I'm not looking to be the next." No sooner than the words left her mouth did she regret speaking them. Some things were better left unsaid, and Moore wasn't the only one hurt by Durgin's loss. Anytime you lost one of your own, it stung. She sighed and spoke again, "Listen, I don't mean to take my frustration out on you, but things are crazy. The murders, then Officer Durgin's accident, and I arrive on scene to a murder I don't even know how to begin to explain. Is Laurie okay?"

The voice on the other line replied, "I understand, Detective. We all do. Laurie is fine. At least she was the last I saw her."

"What do you mean, the last you saw her?"

"She just took off. Put her coat on and left."

"And none of you made any attempt to stop her?"

"No."

"And why the fuck not?" Detective Moore yelled at her phone.

"Because she's not a suspect. Because we aren't detaining her. We can't just hold her here for no reason."

Moore knew that was bullshit. Legally, he was right, they *couldn't* hold her, but they both knew damn well they held people all the time for stupid shit. To make them sweat, to fuck with them. They toed the line of legality all the time. "The roads are dog shit, so how about you hold her there for her own safety?"

"Detective Moore, I know you're upset, but we can't hold her for that either. The state of emergency is lifted and citizens are free to drive the roads if they choose."

And he was right about that too. Although she didn't agree with the governor's decision to lift the declaration, she knew why he did it. It was the same reason they lifted it as soon as possible every year. Money. Businesses being closed means a loss of tax revenue. Cities and the state all take massive losses in such revenue. And there was an increase in payroll too. The essential personnel—mostly police, fire, and correctional employees—all had it written into their contracts that they would receive a pay rate of double time for all hours worked during a state of emergency declaration, which was another reason the governor wanted to lift it sooner rather than later. Such decisions were never truly made in the interest of safety and were *always* weighed against cost.

"Yeah, I know. If she happens to make her way back, please try to get her to stay put. And if she calls the station, just give her my number."

"Ten-four, Detective." The call disconnected, the speakers reverting to the gaming podcast she'd been listening to. In the always dwindling spare time Jennifer Moore had, she enjoyed playing video games. They took her mind off the horrors of everyday life, and though she rarely had the time to sit down and enjoy them these days, she was still a gamer at her core. And this particular podcast went on for hours and made her workdays palatable.

Dammit, Laurie. Why couldn't you just stay put? There was no doubt in Detective Moore's mind that Laurie was on her way to the hospital to see her niece. Inevitably, the two of them would cross paths again today, and when they did, she'd give Laurie a gentle chastising. Tact was something Jennifer Moore struggled with, but she wasn't heartless. If she were to talk to Laurie like a child, the woman would simply tune her out. She knew this because she would do the same thing herself if the situation were reversed. Still, she needed to make sure Laurie understood just how stupid it was for her to risk her safety on the roads today.

She was all Cindy had left.

At least the road leading to the hospital had been plowed. Detective Moore had no trouble with the last leg of the trip. The parking lot was clear of snow, too, and oddly enough, it was practically empty.

"They must still be diverting to the other hospitals," Detective Moore said aloud, remembering the power outage Glenwood Memorial had been struggling with.

She stepped out of the vehicle and saw the lights were on, but that meant nothing. They were on yesterday too. The generator system seemed to be holding up well enough, but she knew it must still be running on emergency power. Otherwise, they wouldn't be diverting to other hospitals and both the staff and patient parking lots would be home to many more vehicles than they currently contained.

Not far from where Detective Moore parked, she saw

an ambulance, its engine idling. Exhaust fumes billowed out from the back of the vehicle. She couldn't help but wonder how bad it affected patients with respiratory emergencies to be on the breathing end of the fumes.

She made her way to the ambulance to interview the EMTs. When she'd spoken with them on the phone they didn't seem like the best of the bunch, so she was relieved to see they had waited as requested.

As soon as she'd gotten within a few feet of the ambulance her intuition was screaming at her. Something seemed off. She couldn't see anyone in the front—no driver, no passenger. There were streaks of something dark across the windows and Detective Moore's first thought was: blood.

She unholstered her pistol, keeping the cold steel weapon at a low ready, her finger straight and off the trigger as she rounded the back of the vehicle. The rear doors were flung wide and before she could see inside, she saw the snow directly behind it was dark red. The heavy scent of blood overpowered the exhaust fumes. Before proceeding, she stopped, tapped her phone, and called for backup.

When she got to the back of the vehicle, it was like something straight out of a nightmare or a gory horror flick. A low-budget affair with a shoddy story propped up on hyperrealistic special effects. It was so disgusting she struggled to keep herself together. There was more blood than she'd ever seen in her life splattered everywhere. Puddled in the snow directly behind the ambulance, splashed across the rear doors and the interior walls of the vehicle. It dripped from the ceiling like water from pipes in a basement. A severed human arm protruded from the tailpipe, blood running down the hand and onto the ground below. The fingernails were manicured and painted black, the fingers themselves slender. She couldn't tell for sure, but it was more than likely the woman, Kendra, she thought her name was.

She stepped up into the rear of the vehicle, her flashlight in one hand, gun in the other. There was plenty of natural light, but she wanted to make sure she didn't miss anything potentially important. Detective Moore took one look at the stretcher and dry heaved. A woman's head sat atop a pile of entrails and organs, a pyramid stack of limbs sat right next to the head, and underneath the stretcher was a hollowed-out midsection. There were five limbs in the pile on the stretcher; only one of the arms matched the arm hanging from the tailpipe. Both EMTs dead.

That was the final straw, there was no holding it in. Detective Moore turned around and spewed in the puddle of blood behind the ambulance. The CSI unit would flip their wigs over the contaminated crime scene, but as far as she was concerned, they could fuck off. It was unreasonable to expect anyone *not to* get sick over the grisly tableau left in the ambulance.

Looking over her shoulder, Detective Moore knew there was more to the scene. There was *something* in the front seat, and though she couldn't be sure, her money was on another macabre display.

It only took a moment of looking around the back of the ambulance for her to give up on climbing from the back to the front. There was no way to accomplish the task without disturbing the crime scene, so she hopped out of the back of the vehicle, kept her weapon ready, and walked around to the front driver's side. She grabbed the handle, opened the door, and the lower half of a torso spilled out. The entrails—still warm—emitted a visible cloud of steam as they unraveled across her boots.

"What the fuck!" she yelled, jumping back. She kicked her foot, trying to remove the organic material and after a few kicks, a thick chunk of *something* flew off her boot, smacked the side of the vehicle, and slid down it, leaving a snail trail of blood in its wake.

She looked up and saw the remaining portion of the body swaying gently along the inside of the door panel. The man was looking down and to the side and a red Christmas hat sat atop his head, canted to the left, the white puffball dangling in front of his face. His arms were spread wide, palms nailed to the door paneling with icicle spikes. The positioning of the body looked an awful lot like depictions she recalled of the crucifixion of Jesus. The dead man's stigmata-like palm wounds wept a trail of blood that ran a river down his arms. On his side, another wound with a candy cane hooked inside the flap of skin.

Definitely a crucifixion display. Who the fuck would do this? The crime flipped her mind into overdrive, making her wonder if there had been another suspect present at the Feltcher house who had helped Reynolds unleash the carnage of the previous night. Maybe. The prospect was certainly plausible. With everything that went down, two murderers would have had a much easier time accomplishing the killing spree.

What the hell had happened here? How had no one

seen this or called it in? Detective Moore kept her weapon at the ready and jogged to the hospital entrance, hoping to find answers. Surely if nobody had seen anything, there would at least be security footage to go over.

Keith Filmore was almost in the clear. He'd traversed the hospital, avoided staff, managed to avoid Smythe's partner, even kept clear of hospital security, then snuck out through the side door. Freedom at last. He could take in the fresh air on his own accord without being told to go back into his cell. He didn't have to worry about anyone trying to rape him or shank him in the showers. He was a free man, so long as he could get as far away from Glenwood as possible.

But something told him to turn around. Call it intuition. Call it paranoia. Whatever the hell it was, it pointed him directly at that bitch detective who had put him away all those years ago.

Keith liked to call that karma.

He turned around and made his way back to the hospital.

One last thing to do before he escaped this town for good.

Chapter Fifteen

Laurie kept her eyes locked on the road, occasionally glancing at the navigation system. She was making damn good time, but it wasn't enough. Cindy needed her. Laurie knew she needed to step up and be there for her niece to make sure that the poor girl had *some* shot at a successful future. Lord knows the deck would be stacked against her after all the trauma she had just endured. Her entire family brutally murdered by a maniac simply because the piece of shit had a bone to pick. Not because Jack was a bad man, but because he had done his job. Because Jack performing the duties of his profession inevitably ensured that he would always have a target on his back, especially in a state as small as Rhode Island.

He had felt trapped. Laurie recalled their conversations in the early years of his career, back when the kids were much younger, his marriage still fresh. He often lamented the fact that every time he went somewhere, he saw former inmates. Most of the time it was no problem, but there were a few times when things had almost taken a bad turn. He carried a concealed weapon at all times after the first incident when he was assaulted at the mall, off duty, by someone who had recognized him as a corrections officer. That particular inmate wasn't even one he'd had a problem with at the prison. The man simply hated law enforcement officers. After that, he rarely left the house unarmed and avoided going places with the family where he felt he might run into former inmates.

No more festivals, no more local carnivals. The largest mall in the state was out of the question. Concerts, sporting events, certain restaurants that were upscale but just outside of bad areas, all off-limits to the Feltcher clan.

But it was all for naught because at the end of the day, some scumbag had tracked Jack down and took everything from Cindy. Had taken away the opportunity for Laurie to reconnect with her brother-in-law and be a part of that side of the family once again.

Laurie stepped on the gas pedal, braving the harsh roads while tears streamed down her cheeks.

Chapter Sixteen

The elevator dinged and Lindsay McNamara looked over the fifth-floor nurses' station desk, hoping to see her DoorDash delivery driver. She was starving and was smack-dab in the middle of her third shift and hadn't had anything to eat since the previous day, aside from the random snacks they had on the unit. She felt bad about ordering delivery with the current conditions of the roads, but she needed to eat. Besides, everyone had a job to do, and Lindsay tipped well, giving her driver 50 percent for accepting the order on a day like today.

The metal doors slid open, revealing . . . an empty elevator. It must have been that man-child security guard downstairs. Lindsay couldn't remember his name, but he was an idiot, and none of the hospital's female staff members liked the guy. He was a creep, a grade A scumbag. And now, because sexual harassment wasn't enough, he was playing childish pranks. Sending the elevator up with nobody inside? That was fucking juvenile.

She trained her gaze once more on her Kindle. Her dark romance novel was just getting to the good parts, and the babies in the ward had all been relatively quiet, allowing her plenty of time to read. The main character in her book found herself tied up, literally, by a serial killer who was charismatic, attractive, seductive—exactly what you'd expect from a book written for the market. But at some point in the story, he had a change of heart and murder was out of the question—at least for the time being—and instead, the killer opted to fuck his prey's brains out. Lindsay knew the plot was absurd, but she didn't read these types of novels for the plausibility of the story . . . she read them for the escape, for the spicy scenes. She lived vicariously through the exploits of the characters in an attempt to escape her boring, vanilla sex life.

Her coworkers didn't understand, though. The one time she'd tried telling her peers about the fucked-up smut books she read, they all looked at her like she was some sort of freak. Now, she pretended she was reading whatever the new CoHo or Frieda novel was. Much easier to lie than to face the judging gazes of the other nurses.

But she didn't have to worry about that today. Only one other nurse had shown up, so she'd basically been forced to stay for the double shift. She couldn't leave the damn NICU with only one other nurse on duty. Speaking of Barbara, she'd been gone for a while. Said she needed to get a snack, but the vending machines were the only option at the moment, and she'd been gone far too long for that to be the case. Maybe she'd stepped out to use the restroom. Barbara was always weird about that, telling you she had to go pee but then she would disappear to the ladies' room for upward of twenty-five minutes, as if you cared that she was dropping a heater. And what was the point of the lie, anyway? She had to know it only served to draw further attention to the fact that she *obviously* wasn't going number one.

Lindsay heard wet plopping noises, like something wet slapping the floor, from just beyond the front of her workstation. She looked up from her book but saw nothing. *Great, now I'm hearing shit*, she thought to herself. Her mother had warned her about staying on the graveyard shift for too long, told her it fucked with your mind. Over the years, it would pluck away at your sanity, bit by bit. It worked slowly and nobody, including yourself, would notice a change until one day, seemingly out of nowhere, you're the nutbag on the overnight shift everyone talks shit about.

"*Excuse me, miss, can you tell me where I can find Cindy Feltcher?*" a strange, nasally voice asked.

The voice, like the wet noises, came from in front of her desk. Lindsay bolted up, the chair flying backward. "Who the hell said that?" she asked, looking left and right, still not seeing anyone.

"*Down here!*" the voice said, gleeful cheer present in its tone. But something about it didn't sit right with Lindsay, making the hair on her arms stand at attention.

Lindsay leaned forward, palms flat on the workstation as she stretched to look over it.

She saw what looked to be a Christmas elf, but a red blur flashed across her vision before something hard smacked against the back of her head, forcing her to crash face-first onto the workstation. She cried out in pain and the voice giggled.

"*My, my, my, Santa's sack is quite hefty, isn't it? It was very kind of him to let his old pal, Sprinkles, borrow it for the evening,*" the elf said as he swung the sack over his shoulder once more, preparing to bludgeon Lindsay with it.

Her head swam, vision blurry from both the impact and teary eyes. Blood trickled down the side of her face, pattered on the surface of the station. Out of the corner of her eye, Lindsay saw another red velvet blur and this time, recognized the danger. She managed to move out of the way, narrowly avoiding the heavy sack which would have crushed her skull against the workstation.

Lindsay didn't know how any of this was possible. How this toy attacking her was somehow sentient. What-ever logic-defying magic had gifted the thing with life must also be responsible for its incredible strength. Who could say for sure? There was no sense trying to deter-mine how such a thing was possible. Survival was para-mount; the particulars of her situation could be debated when her life was no longer on the line.

She looked around, searching for anything she could defend herself with.

Sprinkles jumped onto the workstation like a Cross-Fitter doing box jumps. Lindsay shoved the elf with both hands, sending him sprawling onto the floor. He slid across it, the tile screeching underneath him until he skidded to a halt.

Lindsay ran to the elf, no longer stunned from the blow to the head. She grabbed him by the ankles, swung him like a discus, and launched Sprinkles down the hallway. Without stopping to admire her Olympic toss, she pressed the emergency call button on the workstation and booked it in the opposite direction of the hall, toward the nursery. She'd hide in the dark amongst the babies and wait for security or the authorities to show up. With any luck, that dipshit guard downstairs would see her predicament on camera and get the police here.

She reached the end of the corridor, scanned her key card, and opened the nursery door. A few of the babies were crying but she couldn't tend to them now. Whatever the issue, they'd have to wait until her life was no longer at risk. She flipped the switch on the wall, shrouding the room in darkness before tiptoeing like a thief in the night toward the back of the room where she hid behind medical equipment.

She tried to slow her breathing, tried to keep herself calm, but in the dark with her life on the line, everything sounded far too loud. The way each breath whistled, her heart pounding in her chest, the veins in her head throbbing as her pulse forced blood through her circulatory system. All of it, too loud. Sure to get her killed.

Minutes passed. They may well have been hours as far as Lindsay was concerned. Was that thing looking for her? Or had it moved on? It had asked for someone named Cindy. Who the hell was Cindy? A patient, she assumed. Certainly not one of the babies on the ward.

Her thighs burned from crouching. She tried to readjust herself but fell forward, her muscles exhausted. The metal stand she'd been holding on to crashed to the floor, clattering in the dark. The sudden intrusion of noise might as well have been an explosion in the silence.

"Oh fuck," she said before slapping her hand over her mouth. Did the thing hear her? The room killed noise fairly well, but how could that thing *not* have heard her?

As if in response, the door rattled in its frame but didn't open. Thank God for the locks. Unless that little fucker had gotten ahold of someone's key card, he'd be stuck in the corridor. Of course the other patients were trapped in their rooms and on their own, but Lindsay wasn't worried about that right now. She was a nurse, not a cop, and frankly, her own survival instincts had kicked in. She wasn't brave, she was a coward at heart, and when it came right down to it, she wasn't about to risk her life for someone else.

The rattling stopped. She waited. A minute passed. Two minutes. She didn't dare move. Not until someone with authority and a gun showed up. She kept her head down between her thighs, her arms wrapped around her legs, rocking back and forth.

This time, it was an outside source that broke the silence. A faint crackling noise, like ice creaking on a windshield in the morning. It seemed to come from ahead of her. Lindsay looked up and couldn't see anything. On her hands and knees, she crawled to the front of the room. In the darkness, she bumped into various things—trays, tables, baby cribs—but she was moving so slowly that nothing made enough noise to give away her location.

She stopped when she was a few feet away from the door. Something was wrong. The door glowed a faint blue. The space between her and the door felt noticeably chillier than the rest of the room. *What the hell?* she thought, and then the door exploded. Large fragments of glass and steel flew through the air toward her.

Icy shrapnel.

The force of the door imploding knocked her on her ass. The largest piece of flying metal sliced her scalp, blood trickled down her forehead. If she hadn't fallen, the dagger surely would have gone through her chest, likely killing her. Smaller pieces of flying death struck all over her body—face, arms, midsection, all peppered by the chilly, flying daggers.

She scrambled backward, searching for something, anything, she could use as a weapon. Her entire front burned and she could feel blood leaking from the various wounds, but she had no time to assess the damage. She'd already tried hiding and failed miserably. Fight or die were her only remaining options.

She might die either way.

From the cloud of frost left floating through the air where the door had been, the elf emerged, dragging the velvet sack behind him. He stopped, canted his head, grinned.

Lindsay pissed herself, her mind finally coming to the conclusion her heart had known. It wouldn't matter if she fought. She was as good as dead.

Sprinkles giggled, that horrible, evil sound. *"What do you say we turn the heat up a bit?"*

The babies screamed, their cries unanswered. How long had they been wailing? It seemed louder now than earlier. How could it not? Surely the commotion had scared them, their tiny bodies unaware of the danger at hand, wanting nothing more than the loving touch and nourishment of their mothers.

The malevolent elf rooted through the red sack. *"Shit, I know it's in here somewhere! I keep telling the fat man he's gotta clean this thing out."*

He stopped fishing around, smiled. *"Here we go,"* he said, pulling a large black tank from the sack.

Lindsay wasn't sure what she was looking at, but the hose and nozzle attached to the large item looked like they meant business. It should have been comical, a waist-high Christmas toy standing there with a tank almost the size of its body strapped to his back. But the humor dried up the moment he squeezed the trigger inside the handle and a burst of flame spat forth with a *whoosh.*

The room instantly grew warmer. Lindsay could feel beads of sweat forming on her forehead. Whether from the sheer terror of the situation or the extreme heat from the flames, she didn't know. Not that it mattered.

The elf started cackling maniacally, pressing the trigger once more, this time holding it down, sweeping the hose back and forth as orange death enveloped everything in its path.

Lindsay felt the heat blast her entire body. She scrambled backward, away from the flame and the sudden onrush of sweltering heat. The incubators caught fire and Lindsay screamed, her cries of terror matching those of the babies, their tiny bodies trapped, helpless as their beds were engulfed in flames. Their cries of fear and hunger turned to screams of agony. They shrieked as their new, pink skin blackened and bubbled.

Lindsay finally snapped, her cowardice morphing into bravery. She reached for the nearest piece of equipment and swung it at Sprinkles. The metal pole missed the elf, instead smacking the nozzle of the flamethrower. But Sprinkles maintained his grip on the horrible weapon, and her momentary surge of bravery backfired because when she hit the nozzle, it pointed the fiery death in her direction, along with the attention of the maniacal Christmas toy.

Sprinkles laughed, stalked forward, kept spewing flames. They licked at Lindsay's scrubs, the material catching fire. She swatted at her arms, trying to smother the flames but they spread quickly. She ripped her top off, stepped out of the bottoms, and as she flicked her pants off her ankle, the overhead sprinklers activated.

Sprinkles' head flicked up. *"Oh no, we can't have that, can we?"* With a flick of the wrist and a snap of his fingers, ice crystals swirled around the fire suppression system, cutting them off almost immediately. He turned his attention back to Lindsay and continued to spray her with fire. Her charred, burning body blackened, cracked. The skin and fat bubbling and popping, oozing down her body and evaporating from the heat.

Sprinkles cracked a smile. *"They say global warming is a hoax, but Christmas has never been this hot."*

Sprinkles dropped the flamethrower and grabbed Santa's sack, the red velvet bag shrinking down to the size of a quarter before he slipped it into the pocket of his tunic. He left the nursery. Behind him, Lindsay and the babies had long ceased screaming. The noise of the hungry flames devouring everything in their path was the only sound remaining.

Chapter Seventeen

The moment Detective Moore entered the hospital she knew something wasn't right. The place was a ghost town, which didn't necessarily mean something was off, not with two other hospitals in the area and the aftermath of the storm to deal with, but her finely honed instincts had picked up on something in the air, something palpable, just below the surface.

Jennifer had always believed in her instincts and knew somewhere in the human body's lizard brain there was a sixth sense—the ability to sense danger. Prehistoric humans needed it to survive, but it was a razor-sharp tool which had lost its edge over centuries of human domestication. *Homo sapiens* were still a nasty, predatory lot, and invasive too. A threat to everything around them. But despite their dominance of Earth, the domesticated apex predator had largely fallen out of touch with their instincts.

But there were individuals like Detective Moore—

people who chose professions such as law enforcement, military, and other such jobs that forced one to put their lives at risk—who had learned to sharpen that tool.

She drew her service pistol, keeping it at a low ready and her head on a swivel. By the time she'd arrived at the nurses' station, she'd realized her instincts had been correct. The window was painted with blood and viscera, a crimson handprint streaked across the window.

"Jesus Christ, what the fuck happened here?" With any luck, backup would arrive soon. But would it be soon enough? The department was short-staffed as it was, and spread thin dealing with the aftermath of the blizzard. She wasn't *afraid* of what she might face here in the hospital, but she wasn't stupid either. It was a large facility, and she had no idea how many threats were in the building and no clue as to their current whereabouts.

Detective Moore raised her weapon higher, her finger straight and off the trigger. She had a feeling her service weapon would come in handy before she left the hospital.

Laurie pulled into the mostly empty parking lot and stepped on the brake pedal. She was going too fast, and the lot, though mostly clear of snow from the overnight plow work, had not been salted, resulting in a parking lot covered in black ice. The vehicle turned and she gripped the steering wheel so hard her knuckles turned white as the SUV slid across the parking lot before coming to a stop a few feet before an ambulance parked in front of the hospital. She let go of the wheel and took a deep breath, trying to calm her frayed nerves. Laurie knew she was lucky. How careless of her to make it to the hospital safely only to flirt with an accident so close to her destination. And what if she had crashed and died? Her niece would have nobody left. It was bad enough that Laurie was about as distant a family member as could be, but without her, Cindy would be stuck in the gears of the system, at the mercy of foster homes, or worse, a group home.

Laurie took only a few brief moments to catch her breath. Cindy needed her. She hopped out of the vehicle and jogged to the hospital entrance, so preoccupied with getting to her niece that her brain didn't register the bloodbath in the ambulance.

Chapter Eighteen

Officer Rogers zipped the fly on his BDU pants and fastened the button, cinching the belt tight as he strolled out of one of the hospital's many supply closets. He'd been gone longer than was typical of him; as he aged, he found it increasingly difficult to not only maintain an erection, but to achieve orgasm. And when he did reach the finish line, it was usually weak and disappointing.

At least they made pills for the erection problem.

Behind him, his latest flavor of the week fixed her hair as best she could. Rogers loved the hospital trips, and for whatever reason, the hospital staff seemed to love him. He'd hooked up with many of the women at Glenwood Memorial and again, for whatever reason, none of them seemed to give a shit that he had slept with a significant number of their coworkers.

His partner, on the other hand, was a different story. Rogers and Smythe were like oil and water. They hated each other because neither one of them was a good partner. The problem was the rest of their coworkers hated them both so much, they'd ended up as bidded partners. Rogers smiled as he waited for the elevator doors to open, knowing he'd most certainly ruined Smythe's day with his latest escapade.

The elevator pinged and the doors slid open. Rogers entered and rode it to the top floor where his partner waited, tapping away at his watch to kill time. He noticed the place seemed like a ghost town. There were patients and staff, but the usual hustle and bustle was absent. The moment the doors opened, a fire alarm shrieked through the hospital's hallways, the shrill noise piercing through the otherwise quiet floor. He didn't smell a fire. Maybe it was something to do with the generator system.

"Shit," Rogers said as he walked by the nurses' station. He could never catch a fucking break. Hopefully they'd get the alarm cut off so they wouldn't have to deal with that bullshit the entire shift. He nodded at the beautiful nurse behind the desk when they locked eyes. He'd made a few advances toward her previously but she had wanted no part of him, and as much as he'd like a part of her, he *did* respect a woman's boundaries.

He grabbed a Slim Jim from his pocket, tearing into the meat stick as he opened the door to the room, just as clueless as everyone else on the floor as to what was going on in the hospital. There was a brief moment in the back of Rogers' mind when he recognized it was unusual for their room to be closed; that was against department policy. Rogers wasn't expecting what he discovered on the other side of the door . . . his partner's lifeless body and Filmore nowhere to be found.

Rogers pulled his phone from his pocket and called his supervisor. He was cooked and he knew it. Even if he were to apprehend Filmore himself, the man had already fled, and he killed at least one officer during the escape. There was a reason it was a two-man post and at some point during the investigation, he would be pressed on his whereabouts at the time of Filmore's getaway. When that happened, he would be fired for sure.

After notifying the shift supervisor, Rogers did a check of the room, just in case Filmore was hiding. He knew the convict would not still be in there, considering his partner had been stripped of his uniform, but he still had to check. Smythe was already dead because of him, and he needed to make sure nobody else lost their lives because of his stupidity.

As expected, the room was empty. Filmore was probably long gone by now. But he'd be on foot unless he'd managed to commandeer a vehicle from one of the hospital staff members or patients. At least he didn't have the cruiser. Filmore managing to steal that would have been the only thing that could have made the current predicament worse. But Rogers was the driver, not Smythe, so the keys had remained with him.

Rogers jogged his way back to the nurses' station. The nurse, Liosha, he thought her name was, looked up at him, seemingly annoyed. She placed the phone handset in the cradle and said, "Not today, Rogers. It's been a long twenty-four hours, and I can't get ahold of anybody about this damn alarm."

Rogers shook his head. "We've got an emergency here. Filmore escaped and my partner is dead. Maybe he pulled the fire alarm to cause confusion. Did you see which way he went?"

Liosha's face went slack. "What? No, I didn't see anyone. We have to help your partner."

"He's dead! We have to find Filmore."

"I don't have to find anyone. I have to make sure my patients are okay. There's a little girl with no family on this floor right now. Maybe if you had been doing your job instead of fucking around, this wouldn't have happened."

Before he even realized what he was doing, Rogers slapped Liosha across the face. Her head cranked violently to the side but she stayed on her feet. She slowly turned back toward Rogers, covering her cheek with one hand. She stared icy daggers at him and Rogers felt himself shrink. He hadn't meant to do that, it just happened. It was wrong, he knew. But he was pissed at himself and scared of losing his job. And his partner was dead, for fuck's sake. How could she blame him like that?

"Listen, I'm sorry. I didn't mean it," Rogers said.

"Get the fuck out of here, now," she said, her voice a low growl.

"But—"

"I don't give a fuck! Go!" she yelled.

Rogers gave up. He didn't blame her. He had cracked under the pressure and did something horrible. No excuse or bullshit reason could take that back. Rather than try to convince Liosha to stick with him, he turned around and made his way to the elevator.

Liosha couldn't believe he had actually slapped her. She knew he was a fuckboy, but he'd always been moderately respectful, and he'd certainly never done anything like this to any of the other nurses. If he *had,* everyone would have known about it. The hospital was an awful lot like high school—there, too, it was impossible to keep secrets or avoid gossip for very long.

The moment his hand struck her, Liosha's first instinct had been to pull the penknife she kept clipped inside her front pocket and give him a nice poke. She was so mad she'd almost done it too. Red clouded her vision, and had she not stopped to take a breath before looking back up at him, she might have carved him up right there in the hallway. Surely that would have gone down bad for her, no matter the outcome. The man was a corrections officer, but in the state of Rhode Island, they were legally sworn peace officers. In the eyes of the law, assaulting him would be the same as assaulting a cop. And while he had struck her first, she had a hard time seeing a scenario where the courts wouldn't bury her for stabbing a peace officer.

And of course there was the man's service weapon to consider. Smythe had been armed with only pepper spray, but Rogers was the member of the hospital trip team that carried the pistol. Certainly he'd have shot her if she'd stabbed him. Especially if what he said about his partner was true . . .

Cindy! She had to check on the little girl. She was all

alone, no family, no friends. If the escaped convict had managed to kill an officer without her knowing, how many others had fallen victim?

Liosha took off down the hall, her Crocs slapping the linoleum floor as she rushed to check on her patient. Her stomach did flips from anxiety as she crossed the threshold into the room and saw Cindy sleeping peacefully.

"Oh, thank God," she whispered.

But where were they supposed to go? There was a murderer on the loose. He could be anywhere. Liosha thought it might be best to stay put with Cindy. If the man had already escaped, he wouldn't have a reason to come back to the floor. If she tried to take the little girl and hide elsewhere, they might run into the son of a bitch.

Liosha closed the door behind her and woke Cindy, her little eyes wide with fright.

"*Shhh*, just listen, hunny. We need to stay here and be quiet for a bit. Something has happened, but I think we will be safe here."

Liosha's heart broke as tears slid down Cindy's cheeks. The little girl grabbed her paper and pen and began scribbling furiously. She passed the notepad to Liosha.

The elf is back?

Liosha shook her head. Whatever the little girl had seen the other night had traumatized her to the point of becoming delusional.

She hoped she could shield her from further trauma.

Chapter Nineteen

Filmore stalked the detective, watching the woman check her corners and clear potential danger areas methodically, like the seasoned professional she was. He was going to have to be careful if he wanted to get the drop on her. There was no telling if she would remember him. It had been so long ago. How many criminals had she busted? She had a gun, and all he had was the can of pepper spray that had been on Smythe's duty belt.

He kept to the corners, letting her stay well ahead of him. Something was seriously wrong in this hospital. There was nobody around and the downstairs check-in area looked like a slaughterhouse. He hadn't done those folks in. What were the odds of two different murderers in the hospital at the same time? Pretty fucking good, it seemed.

Filmore kept back, letting the detective do her thing. He'd done enough time in prison to learn the virtue of patience.

Laurie entered the lobby and looked around, searching for someone who could help. Detective Moore had given her Cindy's location within the hospital, but Laurie couldn't remember the last time she'd been here. When she was a child, maybe? Decades ago. From the outside, the building didn't look as confusing as the other hospitals in the state. With any luck, it would be as simple as finding an elevator.

She walked through the lobby toward the nurses' station, the ghost-town-like quiet spreading an eerie feeling throughout her body. Detective Moore had told her earlier that Cindy was one of the last patients who'd been admitted before they started diverting new patients to the area's other hospitals. But something still seemed off. Security was missing and there seemed to be no staff around. Surely there would still be staff around even if there weren't many patients. *Something* was wrong. She just knew it.

Laurie was lost in her thoughts until she came upon the bloodbath streaked across the shatterproof glass of the nurses' station.

She screamed.

Filmore heard the scream and turned around. The detective would have to wait. He slipped into a closet for a moment, lying in wait in case the detective had heard the woman's scream. Unlikely, as Filmore had hardly heard the scream himself, and the detective was a good deal ahead of him. Still, he would take no unnecessary risks.

When he was reasonably sure she hadn't heard the scream, he slid out of the closet and doubled back, leaving Detective Moore to do her thing. He'd deal with the bitch later. It was more important that he take care of this other problem to avoid any future interruptions.

He jogged through the hall back to the main lobby where the scream had come from. The woman must have stumbled across the same barbaric scene he had.

He saw her bent over, dry heaving, a puddle of chunky vomit on the floor. He almost ran at her right then, intending on dispatching her quickly and ruthlessly, but thought better of it. He was dressed as a corrections officer, and unlike the detective, this woman would certainly have no idea as to his real identity. Maybe it would be better to keep her by his side? She could be useful for his purposes with Detective Moore. He pulled the brim of his baseball cap a bit lower and called out to her, "Miss, you can't be here. This is an active crime scene, and whoever did this may still be on the loose!"

The woman wiped her mouth with the back of her hand, looked at it, then swiped her hand up and down on her pants. Filmore almost retched at the sight. Not very fucking ladylike.

"Who are you? What happened here?" the woman asked.

My name is Kei . . . Officer Smythe. I work at the

state correctional facility. The inmate we were super-vising managed to take out my partner. He's a vicious murderer, and this was likely his handiwork."

"He escaped? How could you let that happen? My niece is here. She's all alone!"

Filmore thought about it for a moment. There was a little girl on the same floor he was on. Could that be the woman's niece? "Miss, I understand how that sounds. It was a freak thing. I was on a call with my supervisor and when I came back to the room, the convict was gone and my partner was dead. You said your niece was alone here? There was a little girl badly injured on the floor we were on . . . could that be her?"

"I-I don't know. Maybe? Do you know what she looked like?"

"No, miss . . ."

"It's Laurie. My name is Laurie."

"Laurie. Okay, that's good. Honestly, I don't know. I didn't see the girl. I overheard the floor nurse talking to her but I never got a look at her. If you want, I can escort you up there and we can wait with her until the police arrive. I've already placed a call to emergency services."

"Is that why the alarm is blaring? You want me to go through the hospital with a murderer on the loose?" she asked.

"I don't know why the alarm is going off. Maybe something to do with the power outages? And no, I want you to stay close to me so I can make sure you're safe, and we can get you to your niece. I know what this guy looks like, and I can handle him. Truthfully, he's probably long gone. He murdered a corrections officer and these nurses.

If he stuck around the area, he's a fucking moron. You want to find your niece? Or do you want to take your chances with the storm? Shit, he could be hiding out in the back of your vehicle now, you know . . . like those urban legends? You want to risk that before the cops get here?"

Filmore was laying it on thick, but at this point, it was too late to take her out of the equation. He either did her in now or kept her around to use in some other way that could benefit him. The ball was in her court, she just didn't know it.

Filmore could practically see the gears turning in her head as she ran through both scenarios, neither of them ideal. He clenched his fists, his blood pressure rising, the anger simmering in his body. He was a murderer, had killed plenty before, and would kill more soon, but each and every time he committed a murder, it was something he had to get his mind and body ready for. He coiled his muscles like springs, ready to unload. Cleared his mind of everything but the task at hand.

"Okay, take me to my niece," Laurie said.

Filmore exhaled slowly, unclenched his fists. He had been biting his lip and when he released the tension in his body, he tasted blood. "All right, let's go."

They made their way to the elevator, Laurie trailing behind Filmore, unable to see the shark grin plastered across his face as he thought about how close she had come to her own demise. It was still coming, but first he would use her to get at Detective Moore.

Chapter Twenty

Sprinkles carved a path through the hospital, leaving a trail of blood and guts on each and every floor as he searched for Cindy. It was only a matter of time before he found her, and when he did, she would pay dearly. The hospital was mostly empty, which disappointed the elf, but he'd still had plenty of fun. The fire raged on in the NICU, first spreading through the entire floor before eating its way to the rest of the hospital, the building's suppression system rendered useless by Sprinkles' Christmas magic. His power grew with each death as Santa watched from the North Pole, pleased with his servant's massacre.

Chapter Twenty-One

Liosha and Cindy sat huddled together on the chair in the corner of the room. With any luck, help would soon be on the way. Liosha kept one hand on her penknife, the feel of it against her palm keeping her anxiety at bay . . . for now. If God were with them, she wouldn't need to use it. This poor girl had seen enough.

Laurie stood in the elevator with the corrections officer. She didn't know the man, but she had no choice but to trust him. He had a point; the escapee could be anywhere. She had no idea what the man looked like, and clearly he was dangerous. Better to stay together—strength and safety in numbers. The elevator dinged and the doors slid open. Another officer stood in the doorway. A look of surprise shot across his face which quickly subsided, giving way to anger. "Filmore, you piece of shit!" the officer yelled.

Laurie looked over at the man standing beside her. Lightning fast, his arm shot out and grabbed her by the neck. He squeezed, cutting off her oxygen while he pulled her close. She tucked her chin and gripped his forearm with her fingers, trying to create space to breathe but she was too late, and the man was far too strong.

"Drop it," said the impostor.

"No," said the officer in front of her.

Laurie scratched and clawed but the man she'd accompanied squeezed harder. "Drop the gun," he reiterated. "Now, or I'll break her fucking neck."

Through blurry, tear-filled eyes, she saw the officer in front of her lower something, then drop it to the floor.

"Good, now kick it over here."

Filmore slid the weapon across the elevator floor with his foot until it clattered against the back of the elevator. "Stay right there," he said.

The officer did as he was told, standing in between the elevator doors, preventing them from closing.

"I'm gonna reach for this gun. You try anything stupid, *snap*."

She felt the impostor bend at the knees and she was forced to bend with him. The pressure on her neck grew tighter and she thought her windpipe would crush if she didn't strangle to death first.

She heard him grunt as he reached for the weapon, and just as he did, the officer in front of her lunged at them.

The man holding her hostage looked up and swung

the pistol in the officer's direction. It was now or never. She bit his hand as hard as she could, tasted the salty blood as it leaked from the wound.

"Fuck!" he screamed, loosening his grip on her.

Laurie shot forward, narrowly avoiding the officer. She sprinted out of the elevator and onto the hospital floor.

With any luck, she'd find Cindy somewhere in one of the rooms along the corridor.

Behind her, a gunshot sounded off, echoing through the hallway.

Searing pain shot through Filmore's hand. The bitch had bitten him! He knew he should have killed that cunt. His hold on her loosened and she slipped through his grasp, though he'd managed to maintain his grip on the pistol. Just as he recovered, Rogers was on him, the force of the man's body crushing him against the elevator wall.

Rogers' shoulder dug into Filmore's gut, his arms gripping the back of his thighs. Filmore wrapped his arms around Rogers' midsection, squatting to lower his center of gravity and try to remain on his feet. Filmore felt Rogers driving his legs like pistons, pivoting his body in an attempt to take him to the ground.

Filmore dug in further and brought the pistol down on the base of Rogers' skull, dropping the man to the ground where he lay unmoving.

Filmore spat at the officer, pointed the gun at him,

and fired one time. Blood, brain, and skull fragments sprayed across the front of his uniform and splattered his face. He looked like a lunatic, which fit the bill nicely.

Filmore wiped the splatter off his face with the back of his hand, streaking the gore rather than wiping it clean. He pressed the elevator button again but it was already on the way down. Who the fuck sent it down?

No matter, he'd deal with them and then deal with that bitch who liked to bite. No way he was going to let that one slide.

First he'd kill her niece while she watched, then he would make her pay too.

Chapter Twenty-Two

Detective Moore waited impatiently for the elevator to open. She'd been clearing the floors to look for whoever had committed the murder but it had taken too much time. The fire alarm had been blaring for a while now, and at first she thought it was something to do with the generator, but at some point, the temperature in the hospital seemed to have risen quite a bit. She was almost positive there was a fire. But where? That was the question.

She had to get to Cindy and get her out of this building. If there was a fire, she'd deal with that after, but she was one person and could only do so much. She couldn't evacuate an entire building. Hopefully backup was on the way.

The cop in her wanted to catch the fucker responsible for the murders, but the human in her knew the priority right now was saving a little girl. Afterward, with the help of security footage, they'd be able to put out an

APB on whoever was responsible for the massacre. She didn't like it, but she knew it was what had to be done.

The hair on the back of her neck stood up and her stomach did flips. She didn't know why, but she knew that feeling. Her senses were honed to a sharp point, and right now her gut was telling her she was in danger.

She raised her weapon when the elevator dinged. The doors slid open.

A disheveled man wearing a state prison uniform stood in front of her.

"Whoa," he said, "put your gun down. I'm a corrections officer."

He was a smooth talker, and even with her internal alarm bells blaring, his voice *did* have a soothing effect on her.

But the gore streaked across his uniform and face betrayed him.

The man swung his arm up, raising a pistol with frightening speed.

But Moore was quicker, a trained professional, and before the man's pistol had come level, she'd already pumped two .40 caliber rounds into his chest—a tight, keyhole group that left the man dead before his body crumpled to the ground.

She stepped over him, a pool of blood rapidly spreading across the floor of the elevator. Moore stood in the crimson puddle, pressed the button for Cindy's floor.

She hoped the blood on the bottom of her boots would be the last mess she'd step in, but something told her that wouldn't be the case.

Chapter Twenty-Three

As she made her way down the corridor, Laurie poked her head into each doorway, hoping against all odds that her niece would be safe in one of the hospital's many identical rooms. Each time she peeked inside, she was simultaneously disappointed and relieved. Disappointed she couldn't find Cindy. Relieved she hadn't stumbled across her lifeless body.

She wished someone would do something about the damn alarm; it was frazzling her nerves. She didn't know the specifics but she assumed if the sprinkler system never turned on, it had to be a false alarm. If that was the case, what the hell was taking so long?

Down the hall she heard a shout, an unintelligible sound, full of fear and anger. Laurie darted toward the female voice, suddenly sure it would lead her to her niece, for better or worse.

She flung the door to the room open, stopped short. Her jaw dropped, her mind unable to comprehend what her eyes saw.

When the living doll strode into the room where Liosha and Cindy hid, the child screamed like a banshee. Liosha was surprised. First, that Cindy had even screamed—it was the only sound she'd made the entire time—and secondly, at the intensity of the scream. It was a primal sound, something from the darkest depths of the human soul.

The elf carried a comically large, red velvet bag. Had the toy not been covered in blood and gore, its green tunic adorned with scorch marks and viscera, Liosha might have chuckled. She certainly would have let one loose when the thing rummaged through the sack and pulled out a red and green striped object that looked like some sort of carnival gun.

Sprinkles laughed, looking at the barrel of the weapon, then pointed it at Cindy. Liosha stepped in front of the screaming child. "Hunny, get behind me," she said, just as the elf pulled the trigger on the device.

A red flag with the word *BANG* written in bold white lettering popped out of the barrel. Sprinkles grinned, snapped his fingers, and pulled the trigger again.

The weapon sounded louder this time, and Liosha felt a sharp pain hit her shoulder, pushing her backward. She looked down and saw a gingerbread man protruding from the fleshy patch between her shoulder and chest, blood seeping from around the cookie. She pulled the embedded confectionary out of her flesh, noticing that the tip had been filed to a razor-sharp point.

The door behind the elf opened and Liosha saw Laurie.

"Get out of here!" she screamed.

Sprinkles turned and faced the intruder. "*Ho, ho, ho, you naughty bitch!*" he said.

Liosha took advantage of the distraction and charged the elf, tackling the thing to the ground. She looked up and shouted, "Get Cindy out of here, now!" She and Sprinkles wrestled as Laurie ran to her niece.

Cindy snatched the penknife her nurse had dropped as Laurie scooped her up and bolted for the door.

The elf was far stronger than such a thing should have been, and as Laurie and Cindy ran past, it flicked its wrist, a stream of icy particles flying from its fingertips that turned the door handle blue.

Laurie pulled at the handle but it wouldn't budge. "It's frozen," she said, the fear evident in her trembling voice.

This time, it was Liosha who was distracted, looking up at Laurie while she struggled with the door. Sprinkles flicked his wrist again and a candy cane dagger appeared in his hand. He jabbed the weapon into Liosha's throat, once, twice, three times. Each stab sent spurts of blood flying across his hard plastic face.

Liosha rolled off the elf, grabbing her neck to staunch the flow of blood, but it was no use, the damage was too great.

She writhed on the ground, her movements becoming weaker as the life ran out of her body, and the light dimmed from her eyes, and there was nothing left but a motionless sack of flesh.

Her last thought before consciousness left her body was how she had failed her baby girl, Yanira, once again.

Chapter Twenty-Four

Laurie cradled her niece, pulling on the door handle that remained frozen solid. This was insanity! What the hell was even happening? A murderous child's toy come to life? Laurie never believed in miracles, never believed in the supernatural, ghosts didn't exist to her. But she couldn't deny the fact that she somehow seemed to be living in a horror movie where she was the next victim on the chopping block.

She had to be dreaming; it was the only logical conclusion. She watched the nurse get brutally murdered right in front of her eyes, and oh God, Cindy had seen it too. How much would this poor child be forced to endure?

The elf looked at the two of them and giggled. *"Hey, Cindy, your old pal Sprinkles is here to finish what he started. Santa says you've been a naughty little bitch, and if you don't pay, my ass is grass."*

It talked. The fucking thing talked. Laurie felt Cindy dig her fingernails into her shoulders. The little girl trembled in her arms as the toy stalked toward the two of them.

"Cindy, I have to put you down. Stay behind me," Laurie said. She had to take care of this problem. They were trapped in the room with no hope of outside help. She could try to destroy the doll and maybe lose her life in the process. But if she did nothing, surely they both would die and this *thing* would be free to continue its massacre elsewhere.

Sprinkles giggled and held up his candy cane dagger, the red and white weapon dripping with Liosha's cooling blood.

"Arrrgggggghhhhh!" Laurie screamed as she ran at the elf. She dropped her body low as if to tackle the Christmas abomination, but at the last moment, just as Sprinkles reared back to slash at her, she stood up to her full height and Spartan-kicked him in the chest. The impact sent Sprinkles soaring through the air until he crashed into the huge air conditioning unit built into the wall and fell to the floor.

Something smashed against the door, a loud bang echoing in the room. Laurie looked back but couldn't see anything; the window had frosted over. "Cindy, get away from the door. Go wait in the corner," she said, picking up the gingerbread cookie gun the elf had tossed aside.

She aimed it at the toy and fired. A pointed cookie bullet burst from the barrel and stuck in Sprinkles' shoulder. Laurie had been aiming for the fucker's head but missed. She'd never been a gun person so accuracy was not her forte. She stepped closer and fired again.

The elf stood up, grinning, and the second cookie

bullet struck him in the chest; the impact caused him to stagger backward.

Sprinkles recovered, stalked forward.

Behind them, Laurie heard someone shouting. The door continued to rattle in its frame as something crashed against it again and again. The sound of her heart beating and her pulse pounding in her head from the adrenaline rush was too loud, and behind the closed door, the voice was too muffled to understand.

Laurie continued squeezing the trigger, each gingerbread cookie shaped in the traditional Christmas manner and sharpened to a violent point struck the elf and knocked him off-balance. But the little fucker was relentless. He kept coming forward, giggling and grinning the entire time.

Laurie took a breath, tried to focus on aiming, and squeezed the trigger. This time, the cookie bullet hit the elf right between the eyes, the impact sending its head backward as it fell to its knees before landing face-first on the floor. Its festive hat fell off its head and landed in a pool of green blood that poured from the wound in its hard plastic head.

Laurie approached the thing slowly. It seemed to be dead, but she had to be sure.

She heard Cindy whimper behind her as the door continued to shake and rattle, the woman's voice behind the door still indiscernible.

"Cindy, wait just a minute. I have to make sure it's dead," Laurie said, flipping the elf over.

It looked dead, all right. But *shouldn't it?* It was a fucking toy, for Christ's sake. She kicked it a few times.

Nothing happened.

She kneeled down and examined the thing. There was no way she could tell for sure. They would just have to find a way to destroy it.

A blur of motion and suddenly Sprinkles' hands were wrapped around her neck, squeezing. Its fingernails grew longer and she felt them digging into her throat, piercing the flesh.

It grinned. "*Gotcha*," Sprinkles said, mimicking the Kanye West meme.

Laurie tried to scream but the sound wouldn't come out. Sprinkles' vise-like grip was far too strong.

His head jerked toward her and she felt his dagger-like teeth clamp down. He shook his head back and forth like a dog, jaws locked, ripping and tearing. Cindy let loose a guttural scream and sprang into action.

Cindy screamed at the top of her lungs, ignoring the pain it caused her face, ignoring the numbness in her foot. She held the penknife overhead as she ran, stumbling due to her frostbitten foot, but she recovered and dove on top of her aunt's convulsing body.

She was full of rage and hate toward the sadistic Christmas toy known as Sprinkles. Why her? What had she done to deserve the hell this thing had put her through? Apparently, the passing of her mother hadn't been enough. The world had seen fit to take the rest of her family away. Even her aunt Laurie, who she hadn't seen in some time, lay dying underneath her as she hacked and slashed at the little son of a bitch.

Was she causing any damage? Sprinkles didn't seem to respond to the violence, though she'd carved him up nearly a dozen times. Her lungs burned, she was short of breath. The blows came slower as her little arms, already weak from the Christmas Eve massacre and her time in the hospital, grew more fatigued with each swipe of the knife.

But still, she persisted, poking, prodding, slicing, and dicing. She was going to die like the rest of the family. She was sure of it. But Sprinkles would remember her forever.

She switched to a two-handed grip and lifted her arms over her head.

Detective Moore's leg and shoulder both felt like they were going to fall off. She'd kicked and rammed the damn thing over and over to no avail. The door didn't seem like it should have been able to withstand the punishment she'd dished out, but here she was, out of breath and in pain while something horrible was transpiring inside that room.

She could only imagine what hell was waiting for her on the other side. The saying: "Some things are better left behind closed doors," popped into her head and she laughed. What a joke. Such a stupid saying. Her mind had resorted to using bits of humor at the worst times in order to shield itself from the trauma she'd experienced throughout her career. It popped into her head now because, subconsciously, she already knew she was about to stumble onto a scene that would further scar her.

Detective Moore looked around and spotted a fire extinguisher. She holstered her weapon, retrieved the large red object, and hammered the door handle with it. Somehow frozen solid, it shattered after the third strike. She put the extinguisher down, drew her pistol, and kicked the door. It flew open and she entered the room, ready to shoot first and ask questions later.

But the scene in front of her was unexpected, and she paused.

The little girl, Cindy, was lying atop her aunt, who was clearly dead or dying. She lay unmoving atop a toy doll in a pool of her own blood, which was still spreading beneath the pile of bodies.

Cindy was holding something shiny above her head. Some sort of knife? It was hard to tell.

"Cindy, drop it, now!" Detective Moore shouted. If the little girl heard, she didn't comply.

Cindy screamed and brought the knife down.

Detective Moore said a prayer in her head as she pulled the trigger.

Epilogue

12 Months Later

Detective Moore walked down the hallway wondering if she could have done anything differently. The case haunted her and always would. In her line of work, there were cases that left a stain on your soul, and this had been the worst she'd ever encountered.

She'd shot a little girl. She knew she had been justified in doing so, but still, the fact that she'd done it was something she couldn't get over. No amount of therapy sessions would help her come to terms with it. Instead, she drowned her feelings with alcohol and pills. It helped, but not enough.

Detective Moore often wondered if maybe she should have aimed for center mass, like she was trained to do, rather than aiming for Cindy's shoulder. The bullet had entered precisely where she'd intended, shattering the child's clavicle to avoid taking her life.

But had she saved Cindy's life? With all of her family dead, she'd become a ward of the state. And while

Filmore had been charged with the murders of numerous hospital staff members and the two EMTS in the ambulance, Moore's report had been enough for the state to pin the murders of both Laurie and Liosha on Cindy.

But Cindy still didn't speak and now refused to even communicate through writing as she'd done with Liosha. The fire had destroyed much of the hospital, including the security footage. There were plenty of unanswered questions left in the wake of the Glenwood Memorial Massacre, as the case became known.

Questions that Cindy refused to answer, leading the state to successfully pin the murders on the little girl.

Something was fishy, and Detective Moore knew it. It made no sense that there were zero backups for the security files. Cloud data was everywhere and she didn't believe for one second the footage was lost. But who would cover it up? *What* was there to cover up? And why?

Those were the burning questions that kept Detective Moore checking up on Cindy long after her part of the job was done.

Detective Moore stopped in front of a locked door, looked into the white padded room, completely empty except for a bunk and a small child.

Cindy sat on the bed, her knees to her chest and her arms wrapped around them, rocking back and forth. Each and every day, Detective Moore came to the psych ward where they had locked Cindy away, hoping today would be the day she would be able to get some answers to fill in the missing puzzle pieces. But every day, Cindy looked worse. Her condition clearly deteriorated as the prescribed medications left the girl docile but did little to help her mental state.

Another child let down by the system.

Detective Moore shook her head as a tear rolled down her cheek. She should have killed her when she had the chance. That would have been the compassionate thing to do.

Afterword

Hey everyone, I just wanted to thank you all for picking up this title. The Christmas Eve Carnage series is special to me, and I love this world. But this book almost didn't happen. Right around the time Sleeper Train was nearing completion, I started to go through some deeply personal things in my life, including a divorce. At the beginning of the developments, I was unsure if I would be able to complete Sleeper Train, and at one point I let Jay know and he offered to complete the project if I was unable to finish. That never ended up happening. I was able to push things to the side and finish the book with Jay. Shortly after, I began work on Carnage 2, completing half the manuscript around July.

But then things took a turn mentally for me and I was unable to write. I was suffering panic attacks and deeply depressed. There were a few times that I considered quitting writing, and a couple times when I considered swallowing a bullet. In the end, I was able to pull through. I focused on my kids, my writing, and got back in they gym. My laser focus toward those three things saved my life and allowed me to eventually complete this book.

The end product is something I'm quite happy with, however, I'm not sure I will ever love this book as it is tied deeply with some of the worst feelings of depression and anxiety I've experienced in my 37 years of life. Thank you for reading, thank you for your support, and whether you believe it or not, each and every one of you that reads my work and drives me to continue writing played a part in me still being here today.

JWL

11/21/24

Acknowledgments

First and foremost, I must thank you, the reader, for allowing me to continue doing something I love. I would write without you, but if not for your support I wouldn't be able to continue publishing my books.

Thank you to Jorge Iracheta for another killer cover, and to Red Lagoe for once again turning the artwork into a magnificent paperback wrap for me. The final, polished product shines because of Danielle Yeager and her fantastic skills as an editor.

Thank you to Jay Bower and John Durgin for their friendships. Writing is a lonely task, having great writer friends to shoot the shit with and talk shop makes it a bit less solitary. Thank you to Aron Beauregard and Duncan Ralston for always being willing to help a new guy out. Daniel Volpe, despite being a scumbag, deserves credit for feeding me beer and meat sticks. You have my gratitude, I love a good meat stick. I must also give thanks to Brian Keene for the killer blurb. Kind words from a legend that I will never forget.

Thank you to Kiera for being an awesome friend, and the loudest champion of my books. If not for her, most of you might not even know who I am.

Thank you to everyone I left out, not because you're not important, but because years of punches to the head, explosions, and life long trauma have ensured I have the memory of a goldfish. If you feel like you should have been thanked, this is your thank you. I'm sorry I forgot, I hate typing these up!

And again, thank you, the reader, the fan, for supporting me. Books are written in a vacuum but each and every one of them is only possible because of you. This is my sixth book since I've began publishing my work and I've got plenty more to come. I hope you'll stick with me for the ride.

JWL

Patreon supporters

Thank you to the following Patreon supporters!
Andy
Charlotte
Gage
Kayla
Mary
Molly
Sara

About the Author

John Lynch is a horror author from Rhode Island. He lives at home in Rhode Island, pays homage and always minds his business. He thinks that some people could benefit from doing the same.

- X x.com/johnlynchbooks
- instagram.com/johnlynchbooks
- bookbub.com/authors/john-lynch-2608700b-3091-4ba0-bedf-183bd0cd7cb1
- goodreads.com/john_lynch
- amazon.com/author/johnlynchbooks
- tiktok.com/@johnlynchhorror

Also by John Lynch

The Warrior Retreat

Expiration of Sentence

Woe To Those Who Dwell on Earth

Christmas Eve Carnage

Sleeper Train